SOLDIER OF LOVE

SOLDIER OF LOVE

Michael Carl Bishton

ISBN 978-1-304-26388-9

On the day of her funeral – as to years the life's footprint placed before everybody stencilled the figure forty-two and this tally of all things imaginably woman drummed like a millennium off the one bare number – it was the of-a-purpose yard lying directly behind the great house that was the utterly compelling place. Surfaced in bitumen, the yard devolved off the rear door of the property. Away to the right and further back still was the specially laid tract that she had won off her husband after another of those ferocious standoffs that characterised their union from the start.

Taking after the well of recycling that is marriage, ever reliably these occasions flowered, ever reliably they ran to a script: she required of him that he spend a significant sum, suggestively at the outset, and he balked. Falling to an eventual silence, she left him alone, but days later returned. Now he would bristle, shoulders jumping with tension. Couldn't she comprehend that it was a small fortune? Couldn't she comprehend that his honour was at stake? Moreover, had she forgotten what he had done for her just months previously? Blankly she looked at him as he sputtered. And then, as it came to her, and her eyes now anywhere but on him, away she went again. And after a suitable interval, back she came. The energy he expended, first in the show of manhood, then in aiming his being at the assembling of the funds. In him shone this destiny which is the perennial caving-ins of a marriage. There's the factor also that this was someone who was ardently nourished by the regular daily totalling up of his monetary worth, this undertaken not especially in order to understand his latest position, nor out of fear of imminent bankruptcy, for all the unrelenting pressure from his wife. No, it was a case of the mind following its bent; it was the mind getting its fix in the action that provided it. He loved to do it. The meditation came, so much, out of pure compulsion, this counting and recounting of what was his alerting his senses in a burst, as a soldier will snap his boot down at the sight of his superior. Money, his own, was just immense fascination. Could it be that behind the presidential desk in the city office tower lurked not a little potential for that raptness which is hardly of a piece with the mature look on the person's outside? All this meaning to money, but the eye a man can have for the numbers bears some resemblance to the eye of the minor entranced at what he has found under the rock.

Getting back in force to this one individual, he whom providence had picked out, picked on, to be her lone wedded spouse, and with the sum of lives lived bending at one that fact alone seems to cut him out from the crowd, was there in his view of his wife an aspect that had her as one further item in the inveterate compulsive cataloguing of his material standing? She came with the figure and nearly, but not quite, with the face. These points are made not from mirth at Craig Mercer. Hardly! With respect to Homo Sapiens are not banal compulsions just a dime a dozen and grown man never grown man without it carries over that genius for swooning so indelible, synonymous like milk, to the erstwhile marauder in his school shorts?

In any case, the line back to the precocious one is invincible. Speak not, of course, of the rending nervous surrenders, this black plague tuned to the well-springs of will, the simple spur of mind struck out, the bride melancholy in the worst score. Consort of no name, here and there she, Gillian Mercer, she too was ensnared. But not at the end. At the end the crisis was in her massive attempt at belief, in the massive upheaval of her questing in pursuit of a cure to the most untameable of physical diseases, the frontiers of medical science put under the microscope as with the sheer vigour of her human appetites, crimson in the tirelessness, foreign to reason, she had put everything under the microscope during her time. No, at the end, if it was to be a life-and-death struggle, she chose life.

And all through the three headlong months of that eleventh hour dash to avert, to stave off, repeatedly week to week near on half the length of the country crossed southwards, near on half the length going back, there holding station a metre off from her shoulder, fixed of face, stride vigilant for her first shaky step, he the last centurion, ready, as will be seen, to lay down his life for her.

At length after the day of the funeral, at length following the day of his most grievous humbling in life, a moment of course seeing her yet alive, the protector who had been locked with her down the tunnels of the final stages, Craig Mercer in person, was moved to let out to his brother that he had always been pitying in his view of other men and the fate that seemed inevitably to wait for them, namely the advent of the hour their wives just upped and threw off the marriage, for, as he admitted with about the wryest face ever seen on poor human wretch, not a day had passed in his own marriage when he didn't proceed certain in the knowledge that as man and supreme business executive he simply transcended any such possibility.

What she had wanted in the grounds of their last home, and what, naturally, in the course of things she had gotten, was an open area to a professional standard within which to school horses. Three tennis courts long and two tennis courts wide, the red cinders of the rectangle were so rigorously enmeshed, so topped off in the laying, that the resulting surface could, for the one time at least, have got by as a platform for a contest of the likes of a game of tennis.

Reaching the house from the church those from the special group invited back whose misfortune it was, given the general difficulty experienced of knowing exactly where to put oneself amidst the rootless meandering in and out of the house, to get waylaid by the back yard were at the second of taking the fateful unknowing step across the perimeter driven to grab at any defence they could, the sense immediately overtaking them that somehow the yard left them the naked to the view, which indubitably it did.

Invariably in their panic, the common tactic was to strain for a pose of seeming probing interest in the stretches extending out from behind the house. That it was a posture became, sadly, quickly apparent. These were glances where the essential spiritual basis of the eyes just didn't actually participate in any meaningful sense.

Around the church, inside the church, it had been a crowd and largely indistinguishable. Certainly mourners, but in the situation of the church it was made somehow a professional coming together. Of course, the odd face had lurched into convulsion, but it couldn't puncture the practised nature of the attendance.

Present at the house though was the elect of the day. The kin and that honorary kin a life brings about. The yard didn't merely discourage any two trapped inside its bounds at a particular moment from joining up in conversation, it positively forbade it. As time went on it could be a quantity that took to standing about the yard, yet some quality to the space, some infliction, set them starkly apart, kept them starkly separated. A person was left to himself, the moment one of those when the human body for its owner is just so much awkwardness. No, the yard wasn't tenderness in the least and this was the day when everything was revealed.

Later the residence would be sold to a trust caring for autistic children, they who can, and will, dangle their fingers in an open

flame long past the point the average mortal starts back with a cry;
they who at sixteen, or some such, can, and do, adopt the
alternative cycle of sleeping during the day while turning into a
fully alert inexhaustible presence in their mother's house at night;
they of a scale of self-absorption neutering their reception of the
world; they in their impulse starved of the inspiration to connect
with the lives of others; they so centred their fondness for
existence comes out as a sort of chess that only one can play; they
whose interest in the world turns on what it can do for them. No
sooner did the management of the trust assume charge of the great
house than they ordered the windows barred in the manner of a
prison.

As a cinema screen for the phenomenon that was human loss
the yard could not have been more telling during those hours
attending the incarceration. No one did it pick out more painfully on
the day than the last of her lovers. Someone pushing at tallness, such
that he left behind him the aura of height – he left behind him more
than one aura, present like the ticking of the clock on the mantelpiece
– the yard, despite the cold intent it pursued, at that minute was
eloquent of his stylishness. It was mere gesture, though. The
overriding work of the yard on the day of the funeral was to belittle a
man with his sorrow. Long-legged, debonair, stranded there within
the yard area, this trainer and rider of horses stood, moved, bereft of
footing. Her husband hadn't found it in him to refuse this individual
being present at the funeral. Forlornness overtaking a figure
constructed as if the antithesis of all such apparition in a man ever
more shocking are the tones playing over the figure. Of course, not
always had her lovers been men.

His stables were in the south of the country. First she had
visited, horses a real business between them, though, let it be said, for
both a business born of the big business of passion. Even if in her
case emotional need as easy as not endowed her with a manner like
someone ready with his fists. Yes, weren't these constructions always
hard with her, hard in the conceiving, hard in the carrying out, hard
in the relentlessness of the wanting, hard in the loudness of the
wanting? It does bear emphasising.

She had sought him out for his advice in preparing horses for
the jumping ring. Oh, but wasn't she entitled to believe his tutelage
might encompass her. His reputation as equestrian supreme few
presumed to challenge. She would admit this figure was in her eyes

before the bare man was. The closer she got the greater the chance, surely, that some flavour of the virtuosity might seep into her.

No, it simply refused to retreat this greed of hers to accede to a level of human significance just so much larger that the facts staring back at her on the average day. Over and above all that this image of man or woman meshed with saddle from a certain point intoxicated her. It was as if she kept returning to the image in growing despair. For what remained? Life's possibilities, that which might fire body, fire soul – she had gone the whole gamut. Acting on her feelings, she had tried everything. The intensity of doing was murder of the person engaged in this way. But it was how she took life up. Looking on you were left dazzled, you were left numb, shaking. And a thought came: a man couldn't be like it.

Of course, finally, the hesitation having piled to the insupportable, she had gone to Timothy Farager outright. Here at last was the relief of the deed accepted, this time the leave-taking of the manor-like property in the Midlands, of a marriage, an actual definitive action, of course sordid be it woman or man. Into it had gone the last shred of this woman's defining cry of self, her husband finally upended in the armour of his never doubting, she by then, to an extent, in shreds from the long toll of her insatiable desires, her insatiable desiring, and yet oblivious still of the diagnosis lying not far off.

Craig Mercer's brother has his idea of his sister-in-law in the car on that day, this woman, of defective composure, firm in the thought of the man she was making for, but once in the car feeling she wasn't going to him so much as to all of them, and that feeling evaporating quickly, the sense taking hold that not to one, not to the whole faceless crush, she was just on the road, alone, abruptly a mystery to herself.

If anything is open to ridicule it was her husband's confidence that he would never see such a day. Still, the derision asked to be qualified, for in one interpretation his blind set determination on the marriage in the face of the endless humiliation and abasement she launched at him and their union by her behaviour – not infrequently her shameless cavorting reduced him to bouts of desperate sobbing in the company of his friends – put up the idea that in all reasonableness he should be recognized as amongst the bravest men living.

And, tremendous to have to relate, strange to have to relate, she had an equal commitment to the union. The years went by, the crisis she lived out by the day continued, the crisis that was her own self, never mind, it remained somehow impossible to conceive of her living beneath a roof other than her husband's. As human beings there stood gaps between them undoing all idea that they were ever intended as a couple. Nevertheless, in some way at very foundation her simple physical carriage bore no greater statement than that establishing her deep alignment with her family.

Yes, the carriage: the messages walked off her, and none as resonant as the honour and worth of family, her desire to be the mother of children, the recognition she had of herself that part of her was sent to be the bulwark of house and home. But the spell of that carriage of hers was purely endless in the overtones. And all of it began somewhere: She was it, she was woman. None ever stepped it out quite like her. Indeed, pillar-strong on her legs, often exacting in the set of face, equally compassionate and compassionless, a Borgia as to will, a Borgia in the concerto of body, in the furies of body, homemaker dutiful knowledgeable, and with the ambition for this, and yes, insecure.

So it was anyway until the final two years. By then Timothy Faragher had appeared and all around her sensed that there was a new tremor in her: the tremor of weighing the impermissible. It appeared to reduce her, it appeared to leave her sad, sad like she had never known, sad on a scale that not even the diagnosis, when it came, would accomplish.

What was it with her? What was the thing in her slightly weak pinched face, this martial thrust, this pick-staff of anger, this simmering rage at the world, this simmering rage at womanhood, her womanhood, this simmering rage at the world's infidelity to her, this ceaseless craving to be more than she was?

Well, she did it, she made herself more than she was and the wanton, this relentlessness for the flesh, for its flouting, for its raw carnal implementation, enough not a word in her lexicon, played a part. It hadn't to be shied from. Never flirtation, the antithesis of flirtation, actual like a bar of gold in a vault, it remains impossible to pronounce in rabid denunciation, impossible to have truck with words like despicable, degenerate, impossible in fact to take it as other than a sort of cry in the face of the pain of being, and in the echo of it an especially long cry. The sound hangs in the air, drawing out as if in a physical sense, as real as the train of her dress at her wedding – and never could there not have been a wedding – as real, as lingering, as the wake of a lone freighter in its slog out from the shore, the sudden dreadful aloneness of one large ship frozen through with the barrenness of the sea. In the onslaught of a person born away everlastingly is implicitly the barrenness of the ocean, regret on instinct searching out the sea wastes, bidding the free lonely waves to a sort of final crown for the one taken. But the eyes, hers – at once they were ferocity and hurt, exactly the eyes of the creature whose leg the trap has closed on the second prior.

No, a lasting judgement of pure sin is no more imaginable than it appears meaningless anyway. Overwhelmingly, it's just a single sentiment that passes over one, feeble perhaps, that we are in the realm of nothing so much as the deeply human.

How many times, present with her and her husband at a limited gathering in their home, was Craig Mercer's brother forced to note that the second the focus shifted off her to another present she just proceeded to shut her eyes, a real anguish evident? Without pause, each and every day, this monumental pursuing, this monumental race to be, this manic resolution that every eye must rest on her; and how as to her own gaze, its every pivot burst with her own person; the cross on the hill and perception breaking thunderously to that and rigidly to that.

Like no one, it was as if she was under sentence to experience; but of course not as any tourist, not the world as this winsome object extending out from beneath the soles of your shoes, rather the farthest boundaries of the sensual in man. And yet and yet: in the contravention of her life was a dynamic not to despise but to know. The doubt, the persistent doubt, is in that aspect which was the public exhibition. There the sinning off the beam conduct was like free fall, or at least it flirted with such. The soldier risked turning clown, or fiend.

She, they, Gillian Mercer, Craig Mercer, discovered one of the country's villages and she forthwith adopted the village as outright stage, no less lavishly than Cleopatra. Nonetheless, even here there's a pressure to go cautiously, always tides arriving in the examination, and one of these tides pointing up the determination that beside her the village was pitiable, slander, slander of something in her that reached beyond village, beyond town, beyond city, something that crystallises only when it is stated that it reached to woman.

As it was the last in the stubborn sequence of persons she took to meeting, he who at the internment was treated so unkindly by the hard space at Northcroft's back, he who in the wash she abandoned everything for, as anyway she believed at the time, had his beginnings in a tree-lined avenue, his father's house that white which too easily can advance to some brighter fairness with the house left behind, the man and descendant older by the day. Of course, called to think back, not called, some weep for nothing, not ever. She was like that, but by force of will.

A collection of solid, elegant properties lined up together, should there be just the single example standing amongst them done out in honest white, it can wear its separation, its singularity like praise. Is not memory susceptible to grand white properties? Some larger objects in the remembering just carve out these vaulted halls for themselves within the planetary fields of memory. Once the hole is made there they park themselves, smug, content, Buddha-like in the stance they adopt, Buddha-like in the impress of the portent they hum with. So it is that splendid white residences wage on in thought, this white they have so trenchantly the augury of something, though of what it cannot precisely be said.

Northcroft, the final home she shared with her husband, hadn't this distinction. Constructed in brick, it wore the guise of cold brick. In the image is a stricture that goes better with the function the house came to in the service of the young autistic, certainly in the mind of Craig Mercer's brother it does.

The mechanics of the road Timothy Faragher knew from early on involved residences with seeming liberal grounds at the front as well as to the rear. Too true, the driveways glittered, too true, parklands in their own right, though not any with the length of the private lane the honoured guests had to follow to reach Northcroft on the day she was laid to rest.

In the corner of north London where Timothy Faragher passed from boy to man the tents were full. Along his father's road the trees were palatial, in their straightness and tallness, in the perfection of how they were gathered into long runs of single file at each curb. So very much in accordance, wealth was in the family, and he grew as quickly as any man ever did to a figure whose seams radiated acceptance and approval of the privilege, whose seams were rich in the vein of the courtly style some military officers exude when dressed in their best, whose seams were just razor-sharp with the instinct he was of, riches and the comforts therein the starting point of the instinct. From adolescence there was this firmness, certainty to his figure. He knew the drink, he knew in what it would be found. Human existence was a thing to be cultivated, he was a thing to be cultivated; someone who got to a certain figure as a young adult and went on without the figure shedding any of its concision or uprightness. Yes, incurably a figure of polish, and yes, didn't the dazzling polish survive. It was cement. A definite count of snobbery was to be drawn from the figure, on one day the waft thin, on another more pronounced in tone. But innate grace was about also and this seemed to cut off the snobbishness before it came to anything wholly disagreeable. In fact, snobbishness pitched low became one of his captivations. Was there anywhere, comparably, the figure of a man that as it invited hostility, which his invariably did at the outset, also disarmed? Let it be said, so much a treacherous figure, the treachery not a cruel trait of character investing on impulse his continuing relations with his fellow beings – this will need to qualified – rather there as an atmosphere spun by the contradictory mix of the mystery of his attractions, rather there in the import he grew to for some, rather there in the fear to take him as any sort of model, even as the model was grabbing and not to be forgotten.

The model couldn't have been without the nation to which he belonged. It was a mode of manhood insolubly of the grandnesses of the great isle of Britain. Here was someone truly old-fashioned in the pride he had for the nation he was of. But do not imagine this put him in mind of what society was about. He was barely stirred to take notice. Effectively the networks of the busy and ever serving passed before his eyes only in his calculations of how to generate the finance he required to live as he wished to live.

Like anyone he was drawn to travel. In Sri Lanka once, staring out from windows of the beach property he had rented, he wept at the dark-complexioned maidens in long figure-hugging skirts who at any juncture of the day could sidle by seemingly without an aim worth the price, for the foreign visitor day snapped from its moorings from that moment on. And to these worlds beyond his native shores he was powerless not to present himself as a national emblem. Back within his own land he was emblem and rebel one. In a fashion careful, curiously so, not to attract glare, he was the embodiment of separation from the common order. But with his innate style, fastidiousness not absent where it might be thought that style precluded it, too often glare just happened. Well, not glare so much, just recognition, recognition that he was aloof to his own count. Were some all-embracing conclusion to be attempted in a single sentence, then perhaps nothing could carry more weight than to say that he was the embodiment of a grasped for gentrification, since his great misfortune was that for all the overt material advantage, the lineages of his father's avenue were bereft of a quick quite like that. But did it matter? In the end he just went and founded his own way of gentrification. And, perhaps, a life was in that.

And equally a life cut off, for at sixty he was gone, some years after her, but the wilful, pernicious hand was one and the same, none of it not spilt naked in the word: cancer. She hadn't been here before. Those she took up with weren't riffraff, but next to him it was a definite commonness they emitted, next to him so much fodder. And she had always wanted that. It was bound with rawness, a raw that stung her, blood lurching, throat dry, deserts where the ache was. Stable grooms hadn't to be overlooked, nor were they. The claustrophobia of the Staffordshire village she and her husband lived in for years, the claustrophobia of the luxury horse trailer, a section set aside as rich living quarters, that Craig Mercer made a present of to her, the claustrophobia of the carnal when inside the horse trailer on the eve of a horse event at Goodwood she bedded down with a young female equerry and was discovered by her husband whom she hadn't expected to make the journey, even though the show-jumping event she was to appear in the next day was of significant status.

Along the verges down the full length of Timothy Faragher's father's road the painless moulting of the first part of autumn soon left banks of leaves like dead fish. The road was amongst a collection of interlocking avenues that existed as a moneyed island within the general suburban agglomeration. At that end of the family's own road in the direction this privileged patch strengthened was an intersection that somehow defied the trees, getting to gangs at this spot. Beneath the congestion of entwined branches it didn't escape a definite compress of shadow. Yet for all the shade about, the actual plan the intersection adhered to strove for strategic openness, sheer elbow-room, expansiveness, present in the technical basis of the crossroads, the circling curbing stones set well back, even to the extent of this meeting of roads evoking the harbour-like street intersections of Saigon. Though only as to the mathematics of dimension. Set under trees, to this junction of private roads was the gentility of a cathedral close, the silence and air of evacuation greater still, the wild scrummages of motor bikes, narrow-tyred, elfin-engined, fanned out locust-like over Saigon's street junctions on any day, simply unimaginable. A tiny facet of Timothy Faragher's consciousness was the awareness that his uncle, at the time an officer in the Royal Air

Force, had spent the bigger part of the War as a prisoner of the Japanese in Borneo. He struggled for even a passing sense of an experience like that. He had no especial liking of his uncle but went in awe of his lean frame.

In the rendezvous of five sepulchral suburban roads came about neat surplus plots; within the V where any two of the avenues converged was breadth enough to build. In one instance that had occurred, the site the home of tennis club. Admittedly there were only the pair of courts and admittedly the wood pavilion, slender green-tinged planking overlapping in the manner of the hulls of some of the yachts moored in the Welsh resort where for years the Faragher family had a holiday home, and whose three entrance steps, the pavilion's, went forward into autumn heaped with half-rusted leaves, was a much reduced structure. While he lived in his father's house he tramped the road, he used the tennis club, in the developing physical line of a young man visible potential to give an account of himself in the selection of arenas school and college puts up. And in his youth he did join in, simple joy of the physical no less present in him than in all. He joined in, more he triumphed, inevitably so. And so evidently he could have advanced. But finally sporting competition, man locked with man in battle, even should it be the Olympics, had, let it be said honestly, to be seen as just a lower realm of man. He with his consciousness floated above such boorishness.

Except and until that is, consciousness came round to something in stages, finding what yet it knew. It would be noted again and again that in him surrender, belief, unequivocal, needed to be realised off a slow fuse. Getting aboard a horse, no less a bike – he could pass muster with these things, as you would expect. The beast of burden was one of the curriculums, of the lesser kind, that a family like his put their young through, beginning when there isn't age to speak of. In a half-hearted fashion – the way he brought all and anything into focus – he had kept it up. It was only when he reached the land proper, pure free-ranging land and the outright possession of such ranges the great vision that had always enveloped him, that horses unravelled to him in the way of those observances the eyes and heart sway to unstoppably, and right to the critical depths of a person. Never did her passion for the animals have any of the truth of that which one day would be his.

And really, he, Timothy Faragher, didn't know her for long, so just what did he know, no matter how the yard at Northcroft pinned him down with the welts of his sorrow?

Northcroft was the seventh home she had made with her husband, both herself and Craig Mercer still in their thirties when they got there. With the passing minutes windows in houses invent horizons, the actual immediate visual boundary in view the point one's imagination begins from, present time, future time, past time business the mind gets through not in a minute, rather in seconds. Restless like poison she was, but it cannot be taken that she was alone in that.

As to what houses are made of, the shadow of drama lurking in the air, it's to be noted that neither the first home the Mercers made, nor the second, bore a whisper of the silhouette of horses. But then they discovered a village where a major trainer had his base, his province of expertise not the flat but the sticks. As the images of mining townships in the north of the country describe a style of cramped residence whose resonance in time can seem a calling card for a way of existence, so this Staffordshire village in its founding shapes somehow executed the ethos which was horses.

Unlike in a mining village though, some of the households put up a fight, and succeeded, cultivating a real independence, instances forming where the scorn of the thing backed onto the sinews of the village, the apathy for it, was vital to behold and somehow riveting confirmation of how in their lives men departed from one another to a thousand and more paths.

But in fact another contest circulated in the village, a struggle in which every single household, like it or not, was joined helplessly and to the death. In the vicinity of this Staffordshire village was, somewhat amazingly, a fully functioning coal mine. Each and every dwelling existed in the shadow of land subsidence. This one of the nation's villages had forced the national coal board into a parallel purpose: shoring up the properties of the citizens, and in this location never were they to be relieved of it.

In the village too were white residences. The third and last of the homes the Mercers had along the village's single long twisting rolling lane would be amongst these. They stayed years in the village advancing along the lane with each change of residence.

The section of the lane where the channel of houses began followed after a bend. Before the bend came a long initial phase, flat, straight, that at source fed into, fed off, the main road. The training stables wasn't found until the approach to the bend was reached, the tight hedges at each side giving way suddenly, the lane seeming to narrow decisively against the weight of construction pushing at it in the one spot, the bend treacherous at entry. Yet for all the sudden appearance of brick, for a stranger to even hazard a guess that this might be evidence of a training stables remained impossible. There were walls on view, their maroon red brick as if a plush staging point between colours, but these walls inferred little. The frontages that were discernible at the lane's edge, they appeared purposeless, not so much the launching of a settlement, rather the last standing items of a settlement that had perished. It could have been an open space on the other side or some form like a building broken in its parts. Nowhere was there a plaque. The Kirkpatrick stables were this secret dominion that only those with a pass could vouch actually did exist, that there was in fact a point to the walls, that there were in fact people behind these walls.

Gillian Mercer discovered them. The first property they acquired in the village, the first after the bend on the one side, was in its narrowed down rectangle authentically the mining cottage of the north, the mining cottage of Wales, transplanted. Their second home along the stifling lane that stood for the village was no different. As to the woman put forward by, clinched by, Northcroft, creeping little abodes. These days it defies Craig Mercer's bother to believe that she ever agreed to such hovels.

Northcroft, the final family home in her keeping, was like a ship of state. And the great point of the ship was its officer's main cabin, and more specifically, the great ship's table dominating the cabin. Northcroft was the Mercers' great act of finally bursting free of the village.

The kitchen table at Northcroft was the apotheosis of a cult that had taken off at Evinrude, the last home they had in the village; the cult that was the Mercers' kitchen table. Green fields mounting thick and fast behind Evinrude, it was something like a harvest that was brought in everyday in this converging on one weighty domestic table. So much this was the pulse of the table at Evinrude, this fulsome radiant coming together of a circle of people that the table doubly wedded in telling intimacy, for an hour at least.

In her hands visibly these tables were the fulcrums of lives. Her womanhood nowhere infected the world like the kitchen tables she generated, presided over, at Evinrude, at Northcroft. By these tables the pursuance of lives was enfolded with a crucible. With her present, persistently did these tables give a lead. For a group of living beings, family at the forefront, then the horse adherents, and regularly a mix of both, these tables put creation into these people, put construction into them, put order into them, put the spur to life into them, put belief into them, were the widest succour, were the source of identity. The founding linkages to human brethren, to the physical world, gained their irrigation, gained their repair. Her tables centred lives. Her tables lessened emotional disarray. Her tables sent the living forth stronger.

And strangely, taking her place at the tables she with her womanhood was genius to, a body of people, her people, in a close circle, the naked drive she had to dominate went quiet, an air to her suggesting she was just content to be included as nothing more than one amongst many. She moved and passed plates, her personalities flocked to the simple association. Though, of course, the association couldn't have attained what it did had she not been there as orchestrator, as feminine sage, as definitive feminine source.

Of a weekend son and daughter could be immersed, lost to sight, the tables a hive of horse fanciers, come in from the yards around the stables, Evinrude and Northcoft as homes not perceivable without the stables in their grounds. At the weekends he who was her husband was allowed his place in the core enclave which was the kitchen, but it was peripheral, asking of him that he confine himself to carrying things to the kitchen table rather than ever being so bold as to sit amongst the cadre of womenfolk. Yes, poignant as anything in the eyes of his brother, Craig Mercer was to be found one weekend to the next hovering at the sidewalks of the room, often with tea-cloth in hand, gazing benevolently, anxiously towards the table, the chatter barely ever going his way, refusing to elope beyond the boundaries of the table where from afar with his darting glances Craig Mercer sipped and sipped and sipped, there amongst this village band of horse lovers seated at the table, as he knew, and knew again, at least one, woman or girl, real to her bed.

Eventually, though it had to wait to Northcroft, he got his place at the shrine that was the kitchen table. The table at Northcroft was the biggest of them all and in the months after the funeral he was as ready to be discovered in the kitchen at the weekends as he had ever been when she was alive, but now he was sitting properly at the table, its sheer size isolating him in all the smallness of a human being, just as the yard outside did to a trail of people at the burial. Open before him would likely be a book of roadmaps as he aimlessly tracked the route his son had advised him the evening before he would be taking the next day, some visit or other to one of his friends, or perhaps even a girl-friend. The solitary breakfasts soon like the stitching of a man's life, and no less solitary somehow even when his son was there, increasingly his direct contemplation was not with his late wife, but with the son who more and more was directing a gaze at his father of open suspicion.

It was like they were starting again with each other, the great house, for all its overreaching dimension compressed to the cut-off presence inside it of two mortal beings, lonely, grieving, pacing the rooms, regarding like cats, regarding one another like cats, the leopard wind haunting the soul of the youngest of the pair a keening so eerily far off it left the house and its walls sand in the beholding, sand to the touch.

In this one set of angry eyes, it threatened to leave the father a kind of sand. Something was beginning, because the aftermath to the laying to rest of a woman mounted uncontrollably. In the weeks succeeding the funeral Craig Mercer lost his job with the American trading company whose operating chief he was in England. A mother gone, for the seventeen year old offspring the father set out in stark relief by the passing, drawn in isolation too by the vast emptiness of Northcroft, and then on top of that to the eyes of the son suddenly a figure of the deepest stigma, the uniform of man of the world stripped off him.

And who had regaled his father in such a uniform to the extent that Craig Mercer's son had. The son is the prince, but then there's this other prince, the one the growing son helplessly makes of his father. The image of this man standing in the doorway of house and home on his return each evening, suit to the fore, shirt and tie to the fore, briefcase to the fore, hard purpose to the fore, has surely over time to build a deluge of ideas in the emerging consciousness of the one born of him, the one complicit like no other. Perhaps few had drawn up so vast a person of their father as Craig Mercer's son. He had doted on the figure of his father and the figure was a set of ideas. And in an entirely hopeless house of terrible absence, his father of such immense creation in his own mind so abruptly jobless, a sort of explosion of the imagination occurred where his father reached at him bereft of all credibility. Something ferocious and ungovernable appeared inside Craig Mercer's son that led him on impulse to hit out verbally without restraint, that led him massively to find fault, and on his lips a crescendo of mortal fault. The man in line, as he had to be, was this person he had oversold to himself. Craig Mercer's son couldn't forgive himself, he couldn't forgive his father. In a house of mockery, the dawn was launched at him in travesty, the complete existence he had known and believed in jeered at him as farce. And indeed the truth was that Craig Mercer had never been the man his son had lived with in his imagination. No end of arguments could have been put to Craig Mercer's son but he wouldn't have heard them. That any man was to be undone by the city places he went to to bring home a living wage. That the figure of a man who was justifiably a man had to be learnt, not looked for in any obvious stalwart image of manhood, especially not in the ones Craig Mercer's son had designed for himself. Glory is to man, certainly, for what he does in the loud glaring context, for that heroism of the battlefield that humankind pines to see, pines to salute. But mostly for a man glory is where glory isn't.

Craig Mercer's son had begun a daunting journey, just where it was necessary and unavoidable to stare at the single figure of a man. As musts must the young adult will pass into awakening knowledge of his father almost with a shrug. He is surprised but it doesn't change anything. Craig Mercer's son wasn't like that. In the great empty house, in the great confrontation with his father at the historic kitchen table, the best of them that she had made, now turned to nothing but derisive echo, he was withering and demanding of soul. In his worship of his father, the son had grown to creeds of a man that wrenched his heart out to let go. That revolted him to surrender. He wanted a resplendent man in front of him and the man wasn't. He was just the vulnerable flawed human being that is everywhere, that everywhere works himself to the bone to provide for a growing family.

Except not. He was the bravest man on the planet for he was the husband of Gillian Mercer. Not until the final property that Craig and Gillian Mercer occupied in the village, the sixth house in all they had owned, did the throbbing centre of gravity to one family's existence which was the kitchen table and its society properly emerge. For one thing Evinrude had a more generously proportioned kitchen than the earlier two residences in the village. The third spot they had in the village was not a cottage, not in the least. It enjoyed resplendent grounds. Inside a feature was the wide alcove set into the rear wall of the kitchen allowing bench seating. Between was the table of tables.

This was the first of their properties with an embrace to it that would allow her her own stables, stables true to the word, and she had them, a set of three standing to the side of the two fields lying beyond the garden at the back. Their fields, for they came with the house, and in one of which in the run up to November 5th most years Craig Mercer went to work constructing a mountain of a bonfire, singly, without help, someone who, office-bound in the week, off in the city in the week, never discovered a sense of fulfilment on a par with that which flooded him when his hands were deep into a task to do with his home environs.

It didn't though preclude his panicking if success in the task threatened to go to dust in his hands. Faithfully, it was deadlines that undid him, swiftly mangling his composure. With nothing so much as a screech of terror in his voice, he could turn on anyone in the moment, and the business existence by which he made his money, and hers, was crisscrossed with deadlines from dawn to dusk.

Going out to the fields and then looking back from them to the rear aspect of the bungalow, and bungalow it was in fact, not a house, the striking feature was the terrace that ran the length of the rear wall of the home, an elementally craggy creation. Composed of building-site wedges of garden rock and slabs of slate the dark tincture to the terrace that came about with the different stone wove the perfect and natural counter to the white of the bungalow. To Craig Mercer's brother's mind the bold rock frontage climbing up from the lawn was even steeled with a sense of the resonant blackness of some of the sheer-faced war memorials in Washington, even if the truer allusion should be seen as one of the wilder Welsh cliff-faces, if cut down.

Extending out from the base of the terrace the lawn was notable for the slope it had, an incline that was arrested as the lawn approached the hedge dividing it from the fields. Where the slope brought up the lawn supported a swimming pool. The lawn was the pool's setting, but the setting was added to by the bevy of miniature flower beds dotted around the circumference of the pool, each decorated at its edges by goblin-sized pyramids of grey-black rock, and the pyramids casting a gaze about like garden goblins.

Bulky in frame, squat in frame, the bungalow was, certainly, officially titled, Evinrude, though that wasn't the name she took with her. The name she took with her was Northcroft.

A significant oddity that can't be overlooked is that Craig Mercer's brother got to Northcroft first, well in advance of the time the Mercers of this account ever set foot there. On the right of the entrance to the curving track that led up to Northcroft stood a lodge. As a property, in the market place at least, it had established its independence of the great manor house so quintessentially of a feudal stare situated on the land immediately behind it. Craig Mercer's brother, at the time embarking on his earliest marriage, and not without great misgivings on the part of his city-made wife, had settled on the lodge for their second home with a swiftness of decision that was entirely uncharacteristic. A reason for both the decision and its rapidity was that the lodge had straightaway ferreted out the toll of images he was sunk with from a childhood steeped in the blessed countryside. The immense authority that the visual assumes was also at play in the impossibility in the last resort of ever separating in one's mind, regardless of the official dividing off, the lodge from the much larger dwelling, Northcroft itself, dominating the aspect off beyond, and however the little house was fenced off in its own setting. The younger of the pair of brothers, too soon understanding of the mortal error of his initial foray into marriage, had moved on long before Craig and Gillian appeared on the hedgeless way that carried a vehicle up to the doors of Northcroft, a passage that in look was suggestive of a remote trail across fell land, at the sides the asphalt petering out shapelessly, lying like a spillage as it siphoned into the grass of the exposed lawns. The lodge was the second of Craig Mercer's brother's homes, or was it the third. For sure more were to come. The Mercer brothers, they were property addicts. They married they were soon competing with the speed with which they tired of their houses. They changed like the seasons are discarded. At one time the younger brother couldn't look at the existence of the elder without a lump in his throat, to boot a lump of self-recognition, that early marriage of his, honestly said, so much of an experiment, and exceeding on a factor in the hundreds the one Craig Mercer entered into with his self-adoring muse. But that is another story.

The bungalow, Evinrude, that Craig and Gillian Mercer moved into in the village in the goodness of time was the outcome of a chance meeting. Living in the second of the devout cottages in the village this pair had, somewhere that teetered off steeply rising ground, Evinrude was located directly opposite. Cottage number two in the village it should be pointed out was specifically that one of their homes where more than once Craig Mercer sobbed his heart out. More than once his brother witnessed it. At this stage of the marriage the laceration for Craig Mercer was endless. In a moment her conduct skated off to the unheard of. Bringing to her family situation, unfailingly, time, conscientiousness, staunchness, deep pursuance, she at the same time turned the village, her and her husband's life inside it, to a devil's brew.

The view the Mercers had from the second of the cottage dwellings they inhabited in the village, a hillside construction so amusing now as an image, was indeed at all times orchestrated by, channelled through, this white bungalow over yonder dolled up with the name Evinrude. A field with planning permission lying immediately to the right of the bungalow had come onto the market. In a dominant action, the idea was his own, the deed was independent, Craig Mercer went ahead and acquired the field, something for the future, as he made the case to himself. But anyway, extra fields were always of interest to his wife.

As to the bungalow itself, it happened like this: some Saturday morning or other Craig Mercer had been busy outside at the front of his then current home and in like manner the man who was the then owner of the bungalow had been occupied in the drive of his property. The two had stopped and looked over at each other. The man proceeded to stroll across. In seconds it was done, sealed. It had been the situation that the man was unhappy. That the destiny of the field alongside Evinrude had passed to someone who plainly had an eye for business left him at the mercy of the worst whims of fate. With building permission his, with the field his, Craig Mercer could overthrow the environment of Evinrude at his choosing. The exact words were summary: 'You've got the field, you might as well have the house.' Craig Mercer had accepted. Not once did he throw his head back at the cottage in search of his wife.

They had duly transferred over to Evinrude, this one time in her married existence Gillian Mercer content to be the splendid dutiful follower. But a mystery poked from the forest. No less a person than Craig Mercer's brother could both then and now attest to anyone caring to listen that with a wife like that a man would need a centrifugal energy for money, certainly its making. All very well:

hadn't he though to reflect on something: isolating the houses, drawing each down to the island of its actuality, seeing them strict and true for what they were as constructions of four walls, where exactly was the extravagance in the pictures that formed. Behind the Raj-like walls and hedges on each side of Timothy Faragher's father's road lay residences that had she entered them at twenty it would have been with the tremulous feet of a peasant petitioner. Even the grandness of Northcroft was relative. Yet as Craig Mercer's brother and legions others couldn't miss, spend she did, spend without reverence for man or beast, spend like a plague, spend according to the historic decimations so much of a piece with the institution of marriage. In the ceaseless courting of his lord and lady wife, in the eternal duty to her, on him, in the circumstances of this one woman, a thing dogged, silent, Craig Mercer provided without end. So where in fact did the money go?

Of course, there was the matter of the count. Forty-Two years old and not in fact seven homes lived in, but eight, for near the end Craig Mercer had alongside Northcroft acquired a property in Ascott so that she could be near the hospital in London she had turned to in a desperate final throw at a cure. Desperately ill, she hadn't stayed with Timothy Faragher, she had reverted to her husband. But what Craig Mercer's brother couldn't ever quite establish was whether the diagnosis had preceded her return or whether it had followed soon after. And it hadn't to be forgotten that along the way at different times, when their base was the village, when it was not, Craig Mercer had provided her with the odd apartment, for, as on and off she kept insisting, whatever the official residence she shared with her husband at any one time, somewhere there had to be a roof symbolizing a place outside Craig Mercer's orbit. Woman paired off, woman not paired off. It was a woman's undying trick of the hands, unassailable in the beautiful deftness of it, unassailable in that it could be done, in that it did make a truth, a reality, in that it did make a woman and a life.

And at Evinrude forthwith, in the final evolution of their existence there, he had paid her out, though staying short of a divorce. And after the money had bled away she fashioned a way back to him. Getting so adroitly past the door at Evinrude was just reconfirmation of her conjurer's arts, and not long after they went on together to Northcroft.

Beneath the garage at Evinrude the coal board came and installed concrete braces they told Craig Mercer would hold a multi-floored apartment building. None knew, not even Craig Mercer, the braces he was constituted of in his day to day existence. In name, they had entered the village as Craig and Gillian Mercer, and in name, three homes later, they emerged as Craig and Gillian Mercer.

In a car, allowing for hold-ups, or anyway hesitations, the lane could be dispatched in two and a half minutes, and the lane was the village. The lane was also years out of lives. Summer brave and true about the bungalow Evinrude, it was the terrace that was her preferred location from which to place before her husband her newest agendas for spending, and it was the terrace that saw him adamant, that saw him drawing himself up to the full authority so singularly, so correctly, at the basis of a man. But it wasn't the terrace that was witness to his capitulations. It wasn't anywhere really. In the event he just found himself beavering once again to satisfy what long before he had understood was beyond gratification. Perhaps he was the only person in the world who did understand it properly, and understanding it he had promptly dispatched the knowledge, put it away, cleared it from the vision of things he took with him in advancing to the business of the day, the serving god as deeply fixed in him as in anyone. From the beginning she had him, cross and mitre. She must have known that. If he went to work for you he was twenty men. The endeavour engulfed him. His brother could have attested to that. Plagued by severe inarticulacy, as a man leaving him exposed at every front in his business existence, nonetheless somehow integral to that was this incomparable resource to be for hours on end a force of nature, and this never not a might brought forth by the need to move mountains on someone's behalf.

The toil, his toil for her, flowed onward at her side until her last minutes on earth, and to the extent, in a physical act of pure sacrifice, that it left his own health, even life, at devout risk thereafter. The final treatment had been a procedure of pure experiment. Her blood had been changed for his, with long term consequences for Craig Mercer that, as the doctors admitted, were simply unknown.

Once she saw it the swimming pool in the garden at Evinrude, the last of their homes in the village, beckoned to her like an order of saints. Delivered to Evinrude by accident, this was a female person whose lack of bodily elevation stayed out of sight, pre-empted somehow by boundaries of womanliness so charged it instigated a register quite its own, and against which a scale of inches and feet just didn't survive as a dynamic to give attention to. No, she hadn't height. Prosaically the fact can be set down. But the thing is it doesn't say anything. There was a form, a form with incalculable arched pulsating peaks and curvatures to it. As she came and went, she was she, the inventory its own. The woman was all. It went further than your mind could follow.

On arrival at Evinrude there was water in the pool and with the season in sympathy she swam zealously, in faithful compliance with the command that was the mere rota of the days. Should she chance things early on, at an hour yet blotted with the haze spills of daybreak, the near certainty was she would enter the water free of the last stitch. But who retains a thought of the water? Craig Mercer's brother doesn't. The deep with all the profit to it was the apron of the pool. Equipped with the odd sunbed, the paved area went to compiling the person across the range of persons, the gyrations of human being loose in the single same frame, the span of actresses in the one actress.

Amongst other things perceptible as she lounged full length was the underlying hard edge of her nature, never entirely veiled; what was seen was the undying rape of self, somehow nowhere more present than in this impossibility of hers to defer to others. And she never stepped back even when motionless on a sunbed. Actress, yet not so; a human being's secret sums – in various ways that didn't seem to apply to her. Here was someone who in the counting off appeared not to leave anything to the imagination at all. As Craig Mercer's brother conceived it, the solitary mortal being alive in the world without a single closed cupboard. Yet, and it's the reason for this account, in the face of the flagrancy, the devilry, the indifference to others were there not the promise, the potential to bring her body to the chalice, in the face of the personally abject, she remained convincing, convincing like a knot in the gut. It was woman, always woman. That was the sound of the running feet at your back, closing in on you, chasing you down, hunting you down; and in the sound of those feet too, as it had to be felt, getting ever nearer as they did, this desperate flight to escape the wall of self, the wall of woman.

Continually, in the intellectual and social realm, she had ambition for herself. Continually in her entrails she thrust off to the ambition; continually in her entrails she met the absence of daring to attack the cause; continually the belief that she belonged in the better salons of these narratives eluded her; boundlessly, in regret, she couldn't leave them alone in her mind, the image of these salons and their ways, their mores.

She was one of life's messengers. Craig Mercer's brother believed that a few of these messages reached him. He continues in this belief. And one was this: that first a woman, any woman, is not the parent of the foetus in her womb, but of woman. A woman, any woman, is in chains. She bears the measure of all women. She must be them, she is them. Except that she is not.

As if separately, Gillian Mercer had ambition for her body. And as unconscionable as this quest could strike one, as all-consuming as it was, as fervently as it might be claimed it hit the target, the ambition went begging in one sense, at least. In a woman's quest for a plateau on which to be seen, which will set the imprint of her shape in gilt-edged relief and advance the picture to multitudes, the conclusion has to be that a fitting dais is just not in the regions of a land, and who knows it like the woman not brave enough to take the bigger social step. It can end with her wearing a fracture of hurt. She wore it. The last face she had, the one that on the day the mourners were most intimate with, was in some way a broken face. In the details, it was formed of features in miniature, and in their projection the features got tighter with the years.

But Gillian Mercer's ambition for her body was more real than mere need of public acknowledgement of her attractions. But any attempt to get to grips with that somehow has one's gaze shifting back, as if for reference, to the border of the swimming pool at Evinrude. The gaze has this need initially to find the body as object, and at the edge of the pool it was object. In this spot, on long summer afternoons, she made it thus. Attending college and nineteen years old she it was who unfussily had filled in when the art class had found itself looking around for a life model. At thirty and a bit the body asked courage of those nearby. As to bikinis, her preference was for the colour white, and white was the colour that performed best in shouting her flesh, which insight was surely hers before it was anyone else's. Every purpose was in the bikinis, until that is she abandoned the ribbon at the breasts. Only when Craig Mercer's brother appeared in the garden at Evinrude did she go to retrieve the string, a bloom of textile fair on some, less fair on others.

In the bedroom she was dauntless while naked, but couldn't be like that dressing, even if the one present was a lover, or no less her husband, turning shy and shadowy as she fitted brassiere to her body, inexplicably in the moment, an air to the motion of working her mounds into the deep cups as if of a woman shelling, and yes, at its corners the flesh and blood shape of a woman turning coy, just for a millisecond anyway, a shade of something passing in front of the eyes of the onlooker, come and gone, a shade that was evidence of the sudden pull on her to demonstrate feminine frailty and delicacy, to defend.

But it wasn't display. It was a factor in the woman suddenly the whole woman. Naked she hadn't a thought for it, but dressing she had. Defenceless, a woman is a song of defence.

At odd moments after she had gone Craig Mercer, some pressure on him, some emotion, did turn to his brother in wonder, in sadness, in disbelief at life, letting drop a small confidence. With these random comments, eulogies in miniature, here and there he bore witness to the woman he had been married to.

In time though the severeness of a person lost wasn't especially discernible in the figure of Craig Mercer, who eventually married again. But in much the junior brother hadn't need of the elder's testimony. For he saw as it occurred. Once she reached outside, a blissful summer day tipping off nature's eaves, too often the graces strutted, too often the graces were slave to base rabid self-promotion, to the crude provocative, to the militantly provocative. To the image of the swimming pool at Evinrude, its paved perimeter that is, is an onslaught, an onslaught double treble. All of it starts with the raw physical; swiftly it moves on to her fabulous self-centredness; fabulous, pernicious, grubby. Body this castle voluptuous, body a kiss from Greece, the eyes of the witness did what they could not but do at some stage, they shifted to the region of the body's common gratuitous putting-about, and passing across one's eyes as if gave a shrug: Venus' soul flaky and unanchored like words, without the key to what is a woman's supervision of woman.

Craig and Gillian Mercer: many a holiday they took in the south of France, her cold intent to bake. She mined the sun like the she mined the horses. Let it be repeated: hard she could be, intent she could be. Days were when she pursued her obsessions like battle. None were shown mercy. Not the horses, not the lovers, not herself.

Never did her face show a ton of makeup, not even when trapped by the plangent testing-outs of a teenager, but over the course of time it showed a ton of attrition from on high. The summers backing up ten and twenty fold, a load gathered at her face like a carapace, to the eyes of Craig Mercer's brother, the proverbial sheathe of leather. She was the opposite of a crass woman, but since perhaps it is a woman's intuition that first it is a physical world, there is therefore a clamour implicit to a woman's universe such that it doesn't allow of good counsel. It's quite reasonable to see bottled anointments as fed from the sky.

A married couple with money, the Mercers tracked the sun year round, but the distances they covered on their vacations were deceptive. It didn't describe people in their real matter and substance, there on the inside. It didn't approach her, who she was, not really. Rising at dawn to the dominions of her restlessness, unbounded, beyond the powers of creation to requite, the earth where in the long run an existence was framed, where its ceaseless toil was discernible, the earth telling of a life, telling of its continuance, the days soon unrecognizable in the dull plod of months, stopped at the county line.

Of course, the common fate of most, but for some reason, not entirely clear, in this case, in light of the person being remembered, and that with sincerity, it asks to be noted. To sense her restlessness, the day the sense first hit one, like fate itself, never shed, was to stare at something the mind cannot get past, cannot hold to itself and deal with on the level which is mind. Looking, sensing, the mind as if blacks out.

Timothy Faragher's eventual alignment with horses mocked her own. But no less, an indefinable penetrating restlessness lurked in him, masked by the cool style of a man. But in two areas the style didn't quite succeed as cover, a vicious instability existing in his relationship with his father, a draining instability alive from the start in the relationship with his wife for all that she was the personification of the regal loveliness his young self probably saw as the minimum proper to him.

And why not? At some level this couple embarked on their marriage as adversaries, and both understood it. In their physical being each was blessed, each was of a bearing statuesque, each moved, levelled their eyes, in accordance with the oldest ideas of a born elect. It had to be a competition between them. Existence was Gillian Mercer's adversary.

Timothy Faragher's marriage was long over before he came to this short brief envelopment with Gillian Mercer. By then he was deeply established on the estate of his heart's wish, in some way another sort of man in the absence of his father, in the absence of the girl that any man would have gone to lengths to marry should he have been privileged to receive her attention. And to this other man was this dignity with horses. These heights failed her in her contact with the steeds in her stables. To her was a nervous intensity that prevented it. The horses were too much objects to found her deliverance. Desiring to be something, she just attacked to realise the vision of herself. She attacked with claws. To be what she wanted to be, to do what she wanted to do, she reaped suffering on man and beast. The world owed her. The world owed her. It was there in every reflex of her physical presence.

Not least, Timothy Faragher's resources of sympathy, of empathy – too often as if traces of something in her – came out in his descriptions to his friends of the wrenching scenes of begging he bore witness to outside the hotels in India when on holiday on the sub-continent. He could stutter at the point when he felt obliged to suggest that a small child maimed was a small child defaced out of calculation.

But he hadn't tenderness for his sisters. A man is someone. Some things can be said of him with no little confidence. But in the man's conviction of what is his rightful inheritance, of what is his of right in the handover of generations, of what must be his, does there lurk a person who, in what he is capable of to secure that inheritance, will never be known, who can never even be guessed at.

In a way his three sisters fled to their lives, for once he began his hunt for every last share in the family business, once he the single male child became lost to asserting that status in the way of a fertility dance made in heaven, the core family spirit, this glare a person stares into in from the start, wrought by and testifying to the existence of a unitary thing, wished for, not wished for, died not a single death but as many as would take away all evidence.

One day observers would be able to focus on these four people and acknowledge that once they had been joined in something. But for the four concerned the duty they continued to observe amongst each other so sparingly was dalliance with emptiness. It was dalliance with the old where the old hasn't the faintest pulse.

The antecedents to the family's wealth didn't trail that far back. The surge to earnings that enriched without proviso had occurred with the life of the man who was Timothy Faragher's grandfather. In outline he was the prototype of the short and muscularly-constituted amongst men, the face a thrusting iron implement sturdy and rude enough, surely, to put to the grinding down of wood, stone, and equally at the sides hair slashed away like a drill-sergeant's. His wife towered over him, her signature long dresses overprinted with reproductions of flowers, and invariably somehow imparted with the aura of those floor-length gowns which were so much the light of the great balls of old. But that might have been down just to the way she stood on her two legs. The picture was imperious, from the ground all the way up. In raised heels never was there a straighter back, never was there this set to a back that banished any and all to the margins. Gillian Mercer had it and she had it without any of the height.

Of course, a form like this it follows that Mary Faragher must have had an significant influence on the matter, but it is surely among the peculiarities of human existence that a mortal person of her husband's bodily cast having succeeded in the making of money, the riches duly, dutifully, passed down, thereafter the physical shapes following on in the family alter in cast. The squat strongman as bare article is no more.

In visage Timothy Faragher's grandfather was a furnace of a man. The kiln threw out one business scheme after another, not least because this was a mental universe whose penance was business, but not least also because the schemes passing into actual endeavour a pattern soon got established that saw the projects unravelling before much was achieved. In mitigation of the man's essential abilities, it must be stated that it wasn't just the one time, or the second, that the taint breaking the back of the venture was the basic honesty of the individuals he placed in the critical positions. An example to be highlighted was the chain of garages he inaugurated, complete with fuel stations on the forecourts. He persisted even though he knew what was occurring, and persisting he railed at the contagion which was the common man. He repeated the truth without end: that to forestall the contagion he needed physically to be in every one of the garages at the same time. Of course, it was impossible. As firmly as anything the string of motor garages evolved to a franchise dedicated to the cheating of its patron.

In time he was reduced to starting a small toolmaking company, the outlook passed from ambition to a vision of keeping the frost from a family's door, now nothing more than rented attic accommodation. It was a descent on the social scale of classical pedigree. At some stage the engineering shop was commissioned to produce tooling for an organization specialising in the manufacture of switchgear, and at a following point Swift Faragher Limited – needing additional funding his grandfather had taken in a partner – was inspired to finish a set of tools intended to try out their own design of electrical switch. Convinced that he had something, Timothy Faragher's grandfather set about marketing the design. By the time Timothy Faragher's father took the reins the enterprise was two manufacturing firms, affiliated, and amongst the customers for their switchgear was the Ministry of Defence.

Taking the figure of a person in its ending phases, Timothy Faragher's father resonated as man of arduous personality, moroseness in his face like a great iceberg. The handsomeness of feature hadn't been given up. It was a face forged of broad strokes, there at the centre a nose of low wide profile, and, mystery here, in its profile famously elegant, and somehow born to the thick-rimmed spectacles that became the rule in the space above. In total a face of blunt grace, and somehow in that concluding period a flavour hanging over it suggesting that the man who bore the face had missed out on much that such physical fare should make easy for a man. There in the white house, the turning point of generations closing in on him, he had strained to be genuine with his inheritance. He had been a far from a painless man to be the child of, daughter or son, but at the human core there wasn't imitation.

He had learnt that in deciding the fate of his legacy no man is king only beggar, the quandaries just insurmountable if you were authentic in your loins. The son he had accorded the greater quantity of the shares in the company, nonetheless, a significant proportion would be in the hands of his three daughters. The white house had stared back at him. It was a deed done.

It was a deed that festered when the architect of the deed was no more. A marathon lay on Timothy Faragher's heart: to acquire that which he knew was his, which no authority could tell him wasn't his. Narrow where in the comprehensive idea of him he was never narrow? Hadn't there ever been a family concern would the murkiest intersections of Timothy Faragher never seen the light of day? In the image of Timothy Faragher, there was the cavalier man, there was the fastidious man. Choose, but do not choose, because the one was the other. He got his fastidiousness from his father. It might have left him accepting of the terms of his father's will, it might have had him revolting against them. He revolted.

Three sisters he had when he started the marathon, and not a one not possessed of looks. Including the parents there were the six of them in all and the vein that was looks didn't falter anywhere amongst them. This one family unit was a fortress in the irrepressibility of the fine physical structures on show, as if of right.

In respect of his sisters this shouldn't be taken as indicating startling faces, rather faces to be given their due. If one of his sisters had been granted a face with a stride going further than notable attractiveness, it was the eldest of the three. Actually, Morgan was the eldest outright, for he, Timothy, came second. She was also the tallest of the four children, edging him. She had shoulders too, a definition against which his nattiness of body could be found wanting. Timothy Faragher: trim was the form, trim was the walk. Morgan Faragher: strength of structure, as clearly in the face as anywhere, an aspect apparent to her features intrinsically sculpture. That is, in the way that Ava Gardner's face was purely sculpture. In fact, Morgan shared more than the famous image's power of curvature, between the two faces a definite likeness was in play too. It's a conception that is embroiled with the hair. Adorning Morgan's face, cradling her face, spotting as counterpoint the regal marble whites of the face, was certainly the raven black locks of legend. Of the four children she was the one who was capped. Compulsively the head was with mane and in the glory of it was coronet. All in all, it was a face of handsome soldierly bumps, the nose with its strong flanks the party piece. It could be said the nose was like the strongest of chins. The terrific edge in the face wasn't anything to do with the dead to a point razor-like summits a diamond cutter brings about with his work but with crests that have been deflowered, wide sonorous curves placed about. That's it really: Morgan Faragher's sonorous beauty. And always, for a face is never not the continuing expression of some singular factor appertaining to it, where it in fact exists, it was a face framed by the handsomeness of the jawbone, singled out by the handsomeness of the jawbone, a score to that shape carrying all before it. It was the father's face, but recast as woman.

In its links the face of the second of his sisters observed structures more in keeping with the mother's. As to some extent did Timothy Faragher's. The groundwork was tighter. A form projecting, it did it more abruptly, a clipped camber the final product.

Nonetheless, across Piper's face, as with all six of them, at the junctures where the bevels blended the coming together realized mellifluousness of line. It didn't prevent the tremulous being present in the mother's face almost as a voice. In her features too Piper was infected, but the eddy of it was quieter. Of the six of them, Piper was the most sheerly intense in visage, like a pending bitterness at life before any worthwhile body of experience has been accumulated.

To the youngest of Timothy Faragher's sisters, Ruth, was a ladle of a face, a ladle tipping softness at the world, all of this gush, this sentience, executed by a web of curves and domes as tender as milk. It could have been decided that the eyes followed from this, it could have been decided that the eyes were the premise from which everything took off, that they were mother to the whole. In any case in this person the eyes officiated, and grandly, for the eyes were something of a river in flow. Even if in passing a capacity, and willingness, existed for amusement at the expense of others, for thoughtless words, words that might stab, and out of unconscious ambition that they should, at source was a blameless heart, without conception of, much less impulse for, bare cruelty.

It beseeches one to suggest that Ruth Faragher was someone whose business with the world was lastingly, exceedingly, in the realm of woman. But straightaway it's a statement that brings on itself the image of Gillian Mercer. The compass that is woman: it incurs Gillian Mercer, it incurs others, amongst whom is Ruth Faragher. As to cost to a person, cost as in reverberation that reaches to the well-springs, it is surely not men women suffer but they who bodily are in their image.

Timothy Faragaher rebelled against his father's will. A fire was lit, Morgan, Piper, Ruth, the targets. He proceeded according to an unfolding ideology of entitlement, the reasoning sealed no sooner than it appeared to him, beginning with the glaring undeniable reality of the company's future depending on the son; which in the stating of this to himself took as read the succeeding argument that where sole responsibility lies with a person it confers incontrovertible sanction, right; the right to attest that the idle and non-contributing, especially if they were sisters, would not have their pockets lined by the one who has to put in the day to day labour; the right to point out the obvious that in a situation of three sisters incontrovertibly there would soon be three husbands; the right to point out that a product of their inevitable marriages would be his hopelessness in ever understanding who in fact he was reporting to in the annual explanation of the firm's affairs; the right to address the destruction that waited for the company when the time arrived for them to make out their own wills, since a commercial organization could live with a million shareholders, but it could not live with one hundred if they were of the same clan.

Of course, making out his case, righteous man rising up in a room like a lighthouse, he never lost sight of the consideration that the ideas he had for his life would demand he withdraw sums from the company that alone, given that the salaries of the employees would have to be found week to week, would likely leave the organization existing at the edge. Accepting the amounts he anticipated needing, there wasn't the room for a broader munificence.

It was a family but in circumstances where this described an imbalance between the heirs, male presence in relation to female presence, active in relation to passive, what he met in himself was the impossibility of sharing the commercial enterprise that the father had ceded to his offspring. It seemed that impossibility made of a man what it would, even though there was the person who came before, and no less another still to materialize after. He proceeded according to the well-recorded odyssey whereby a man remains a stranger to an hour's rest until the hour will dawn assuring him that the prize is his.

Jointly with all of this he submitted to his friends' insistence that he have a stag party. At the city bar on the night they barracked him as if he were cattle. Having deprived him of everything he stood in, vest and pants included, he was driven up onto a table-top. They hadn't planned he should reign there alone. Facing him, inches away and as nude as he was, as upright as he was, was the whore who had been engaged for the evening. The bar wasn't empty. Timothy Faragher was a star. He hadn't to do a thing in the world for this to be the reality. He and the whore were penned in, a sea of inglorious faces staring up at them from the floor. Of course, everyone in the bar remained blank as to what any of it was supposed to achieve.

Needless to say a night's auction of male boisterousness was to no ultimate avail. Two looks were condensed into his face, impassive and subdued as he was inside the raucous slovenly crowd of his confederates. One in passing was directed at the female in front of him. It said he wouldn't touch her with a barge-pole. But the balance of what lay in his face wasn't for the whore but for his friends, and the balance was pity. And the pity was truth for revelation came with it: that it wasn't just his unconscious conviction that his friends were lesser mortals, he bore the belief like a pocket mirror he kept lifting to his eyes

And yet there was sadness too in his own knowledge of his exception. That in the final resort he would be prevented from closing the last of the distance between him and that bunch of his friends circled around the table at his stag night do filled him with regret. Somehow he didn't quite understand it, this difference of his. He passionately wanted to be different, but somehow he spent his whole life trying to explain to himself why he was. The squire with his fawning entourage, and needing them, yet the outsider.

The whore, in days not to be so much the buried past as the past flown, was a blonde, but her hair had none of the crisp register of the straw-coloured hair belonging to the girl he was to rendezvous with at the church in the morning; she of an appearance so terrifically the embodiment of a peerless disinterest in complication.

In her way, an angel walked an angel whose quilt was naturalness. The flesh of the land, the flesh of the trousers and jackets he tried on in the shops and stores, the flesh of woman, Timothy Faragher's eye was for the perfect. He never succeeded like he succeeded in the girl he found to be his wedded wife.

To get to the point of speaking the words, he hesitated, as before him his father had hesitated. But probably that he would propose to her had never been in doubt. Still, with this quality and style each was drenched in, in advancing the critical last metre to each other it was a battle of souls that came before and a battle of souls they went forward to.

But no one can think that Timothy Faragher was wracked at the prospect. It is hard to believe that Timothy Faragher was ever wracked of mind, at least not until the realization of physical affliction in the last year. Perhaps, though, this had been greeted impassively. The soulless obsession that overtook him as a result of his poor father's attempt at fairness with a legacy, his terrible faltering in the yard at Northcroft, have to be embraced as exception.

In body his grandfather had been the template of the street scrapper, the burly engine room hand stoking the ship's furnace. Timothy Faragher's heat was its perfect absence. The imprint of him in the mind is sleekness of manhood the imprint is swish blue blood composure, somewhere in a figure's innate grooming the trail of an imperishable ancestral hauteur, as a demeanour not dissimilar to that of the tall, straight, rod-slender trees arrayed like sentries down the length of his father's road. This is not a charge against him, just an attempt to negotiate the essential remoteness he gave off. Somewhere he was a den of secrecy, and the gates were as formidably closed at sixty as they were at twenty.

The girl he chose to wed was to be negotiated, and with care at each and every step. The half-circle of straight hair was finished to a length, that suspended bowl-form it held to its religion. Everything was discernible on the day because she had chosen to abhor any sort of shroud of gossamer about her head. What went with her grace was the reined back, the harsh censoring of adornment. The touches she applied played to the creature that nature had invented and worked; and with her nature had chosen to make its appearance in the world without the swaddling clothes. She was the austere princess, the glow of her beauty a manifestation of being intensely spartan somehow as to physique and complexion.

Where she went with herself in calculation of the image to create and invest in ordained an everlasting cleanness of look. And the conviction was dead on. Nature never worked anything as purely fresh in look as her. To tamper was sacrilege; so quintessentially, a bare head, this was she.

Down through the generations Timothy Faragher's family bore the seal of wives taller than the men. In the event he strengthened the habit. The girl he had found came to the church fallow in her height, in her carriage; fallow and reckless. Perhaps without the recklessness she wouldn't have agreed to this man. Of course, a hundred others would have gone in her place in a second. But the point was she hadn't to be included with any hundred or even any five. Who was she but a girl who came as she was and wasn't this 'was' blessing incarnate. The throat when lifted up was extension near to ballet. The climbing line of the figure brought the thought of a tendril. The laugh was nature's iridescence and in the sound was both the confidence of what she knew she had and her crazy astonishment that this was in fact her image, her movement over the earth. She didn't quite know how to meet her beauty. Her way found her careless, but there was an edge of fear in this that the gods were demanding she concentrate more for what they had dared to pass to her.

Wearing the freer of her skirts they swirled, and with this arching rustle of her clothes out to the side the girl turned coltish, wherein to perfection was the name she had: Harriet.

From the church the couple went to a life centred at the beginning on a house in the King's Road. Eventually it would be Harriet's out and out. The marriage was sustained beyond the adolescent years of the two daughters they had. It survived beyond his discovering the landed estate of his heart, these downs located in the deepest recesses of Berkshire. In time the businesses were sold. But until that day they did him proud, serving him in the manner accorded to a gentleman.

And a gentleman was pitiless. Arriving in the King's Road he was scathing in his view of the 'system'. With their thankless monotony the daily patterns that had had the allegiance of his father and grandfather to him appeared some shed of existence. The shed told of that estimable figure who was regular man, regular citizen of nation and country doing his bit; it told of the office the poor fool gave himself up to for the better part of his days; it told of the drab dreary corridors outside the office; it told of a man going between meetings; it told of the gift of days on earth being lost to death; it told of dead men addressing print-outs, dead men slaving over the construction of those printouts; it told of a man taking excursions to the factory floor to consult with foremen; it told of the purlieu of the masses; it told of the crushing lives of the masses; it told of ciphers; it told of one more of these ciphers crossing the parking lot in the evening to find his car; it told of the idiotic back and forth across a city morning and evening and endlessly on; it told of a man trapped to the common routine of family's bread-winner; it told of his total contempt for any of it.

But what the shed gave onto also was the understanding that men would be only too pleased to follow this path if you paid them to. So that finally in the image of the shed was the proof that there was a way both to be true to his inheritance and to himself. Wasn't the best of his father's legacies the first-rate people the two manufacturing companies enjoyed? If he accurately discerned the need and thereupon accurately matched the person to the need, he couldn't go wrong; however ultimately responsible, at the physical level the owner might be free as a bird. The necessary arts could be practised at a distance, at a remove. And the arts had their attraction; to forge the parameters, to determine the course, to conceive the plan; to be the visionary; to be the font of the visions; to be the voice of those visions calling out the goals they put up; to be the one reported to; to enshrine the palace in the background; to enshrine the authority in the palace; to enshrine the identity no workforce could be without to thrive in its mission to produce.

Every reason had been in his desperate charge for every last share in the company. The company was the secret to everything; his real ambition to create a charmed circle of the shires and thereafter to preside over it; to preside over it in the action of standing astride rolling green acres a man held to him like he was branding a calf; in the action of commanding that those who formed his flock present their good persons at a given time on a given day, and exactly at the point from where his veldts streamed forth; in the action of leading the good band out across the fields and woods, often on a shoot; in the action of urging his troops towards the lilting interactions between man and the natural landscape that alone were consummation of the life given, that alone were possessed of worth, of significance, of purity.

And in all of it he was successful. But for the existence he dreamed of to commence he had first to realise the land. The businesses he had got from his father, not forgetting the role his sisters had in the consolidation of an inheritance, formed the tool that gave it to him.

The idea of pastures true to the crop-flood they could make real had from the start constituted his founding point of contact with existence. And at the places the acres he went on to control weren't worked for yield he set down beast, really in the beginning a secondary activity. To complement the horses he constructed paddocks, jumping rings, dressage arenas. He went to trying out the European competitive circuit. And what happened but he triumphed. In his country manor he assembled a trophy rack as if out of trophies. These separated-off titans of houses singed by the aura of fields and the outline of the one animal, many are there amongst them whose walls at the living areas, no less the tackle rooms, flash with reams of rosettes. Though he didn't bother. The shelf of plated metal cups was enough. It was too easy. His adoption of the saddle was holiness in the current it made.

Surely no one understood better than he did that she was bereft of any such gift, for all that their involvement with each other was short-lived. Invited over on occasion to his elder sibling's place, be it Evinrude, or later Northcroft, making his way to the stables, a single glance was sufficient for Craig Mercer's brother, a strict ignoramus in the vicinity of horse-flesh. But what Timothy Faragher would never have suspected, what would have astonished him, was that Craig Mercer was every bit the rider he was. Climbing to the only victor's berth worth the salt, the feel for the throne fell as naturally to Craig Mercer as it did to Timothy Faragher.

In his heart Craig Mercer's brother bore the truth like a scalpel for he had seen his brother's talent. Broken down to the elements, it came out a match between the two men: walker on water for walker on water, hands of grief for hands of grief, Pharaoh's grip for Pharaoh's grip, lyric slackness for lyric slackness, pulse of iron for pulse of iron, American Indian for American Indian.

In his heart Craig Mercer's brother was sad for his sibling. As with Timothy Faragher, the elder Mercer had been placed atop a steed while still a child in arms. And when he married it stopped dead. It ended like a life ends. He was with wife and to a village lying like a flurry of twigs man and woman came. Opening from the village on all sides was an outback of meadows, though no outback for this was land tame to the touch, fertile, but in its good order brought to its knees. And in the eventuality, Gillian Mercer starting a mythic investigation centred on this story which was man and horse, never, not once, did husband and wife embark on those fields side by side aboard the majestic creatures. Say it sharp and it draws the matter clean and profound: they never went out riding together.

It was a marriage of no shadows, it was a marriage all shadow. In the historic dark of what in the end any marriage is made of precisely, the shade that Craig Mercer suffered throughout his marriage stood out for all to behold. He entered the shade, slipped out, then entered again. Away from his duties for the American conglomerate, it was his existence. Too many days he was the figure in the corridor, called on, not called on. In any case, horses were the light, and that wasn't to be offered up to Craig Mercer's light, which he had, especially not that part of his light which was his special aptitude in the sphere of a saddled-up horse. The evidence was she recoiled from the image of her husband riding for there was silk in the image, a fluency simply beyond her. She must have seen once, and seeing she had fought against ever confronting the vision again.

What eyes she wanted from the world. It put the world to the test to discover such eyes. The war she waged to ensure her prominence in the sight of all humankind. But, of course, day to day, humankind was the street outside. That someone, in what they did, might take away from her: this prospect was the Satan at large in the world, at large in the street. Ah, but the soldier she was in her unending determination to achieve magnificence astride a horse, in the pure belief that magnificent she was. Did she know? Fixed to saddle there was something wrong. The symmetry, the suppleness, the flowing intercourse, it simply wouldn't settle to her.

The failure didn't imperil she who was the woman though. Waiting to board, braced on her legs, flared riding breeches like flags of concupiscence, fuse to the murder that would move to rip them off her, the horses themselves might have been something from the nursery.

Just the one time she was compelled to return to the image that haunted her; just the one time in their union did Craig Mercer take to the stirrups, jockey and cavalry officer merged. It was at a county show. She was slated to compete in the jumping event. The grooms led her horse from the box, the grooms prepared the horse, the grooms, work finished, held still, waiting for the entrance, and when she did appear what was there to do but admire. The white breeches, the tall shining black boots, as if honed metal cylinders, climbing to just below the knees, the superbly cultured black coat, buttoned for the best coming out, the black cap some nugget of snappishness, the picture was perfection.

The horse was blind to it, deep in whatever world it was in, and like that the terrible set-to had begun, horse pitted against the human personage it carried. With a distance to go to reach the ring, the four legs of the horse were old in their purpose, were bland in their purpose, that purpose to go nowhere, not with this rider it seemed. Its utterly dejected stance couldn't hide that it was drawn up throughout in absolute resistance. It was rooted, a rock in its refusal to shift a single one of its leg a single inch. Soon in her frustration she wasn't in charge of her person, pummelling away in a manner that removes the woman from a woman and the man from a man. She pummelled with the reins, she pummelled with the heels of her boots, she pummelled with the leather crop she had. The rock was impervious. The rock stayed rock. The grooms approached to lead the horse by the tackle. She shrieked at them to stay back, shrieked, the veins in her neck as stark and telling as lather at the mouth of one insane.

There were other vans strewn about the field, each a sort of moon, each with its pool of good human folk and most of these people were watching. At the sides, in the shade he took around with him, Craig Mercer had waited, and then in a single second, before all, the shade was demolished. Before all, he took hold of the marriage and broke it over his knee. As in a second a house can go up in flames, the word was his, the governance was his. He didn't speak, he commanded, monumentally. Two words only: Get down! And yes did she?!

As he was in his casual clothes Craig Mercer went up to the horse, placed a hand on the horn of the saddle and in a single stroppy action vaulted into the saddle like a rodeo star. Instantly the mount beneath him was at peace. He had hardly picked up the reins and the horse loped off easy as pie, the gallows of its former obstinacy nowhere in sight, its flanks pitching no less than the sea's surface pitches, and as an adolescent hadn't Craig Mercer, his younger brother beside him, fearful like nothing, brought a small boat home from a bay turning not angry but deadly.

She had followed on foot behind, all the way to the ring, the riding stick in her hand, gripped fiercely, a dead wand, despair and futility the only note it had. Trailing behind as she did, it was then that the information passed into the eye that she was a woman short in physical stature.

Of this sentient captivity with horses there wasn't the first suspicion inside the house where their married existence pushed off. Craig and Gillian Mercer embarked on the union of loving inscription with exemplary modesty as to a residence to live in. Strict to a verse, suburbia's perfectly bland regimentation, these were walls shorn of nuance, except in the suggestion, since after all there she stood in the doorway of the house, fresh clean young emblematic, the flower of the new marriage, that this was a woman descended from the true blue sisterhood of legendary repute, not one here who wasn't beacon, the cement of a society.

Craig Mercer's brother didn't know anything then. Taking in his elder sibling's start-out property he was helpless not to let it speak to him blessedly, of the said society, of its institutions, of human beings, of the fair sex. A mute cub at his brother's side, he accepted every blissful narrative in circulation. He looked at this young woman in the doorway and believed. A species did exist. It was there to answer a call, the summons to be virtue's tremulous spine, seal of hearth and home, foundation of man and all his works, God's wax cometh in lace. Wasn't it a race whose reality and destiny was evinced not a little by the district's junior school teachers' vital sonorous chanting of certain homilies to the new flock in the class: two plus two equals four, three plus three equals six, four plus four equals eight.

And, fantastically, unforgettably, Craig Mercer's brother wasn't altogether to be ridiculed for his naivity. She was of the sisterhood. But being of it didn't cut the cloth as legend put out, it didn't cut it in any fashion, it didn't establish the first thing about a human person. The plinth was virtue and it wasn't. The plinth discovered for real was virtuous woman's cloven foot.

The figurine of a house had it all, the city peripheries, specifically its lilywhite portions, the city Birmingham in the instance, freshness, ineffable orchestration in its setting. What it had was the gift-wrapped look of new pocket-sized houses built to a formula and making up a vestal row of like creations, not one without a toy drive where one of the two cars stayed out at night. What it had, house and road, was the exact outline of that which she had known all her twenty one years or so, different only in that her parent's road belonged to one of the lustreless market towns that proliferate in the fall-out from Birmingham. What it had, yes, was said junior school teacher's peerless incantation. And as the sound could leak onto the pavement, why not say it again: two plus two equals four, three plus three equals six and four plus four equals eight. Wasn't it a litany self-prophesying of the eventuality of an actual child, so that what the house had also was the regulation photograph of said brother standing in the toy drive holding the toy form of foundling offspring? Of the two they had the boy came first, the girl later.

A house tied with a bow and included with the gift wrapping on some evenings was this steel of hers to listen unhearing to the wailing of her first child in the upstairs bedroom while enfolding her husband with a gaze that told him not to even think of it. Where he was seated he most certainly would remain seated.

It was a scene occasionally played out in front of Craig Mercer's brother. He was surprised and, innocent as it should not be forgiven, years younger than his sibling, never forgot. But while it left him restless in himself forever after, essentially surprise it refused to go beyond. Remembering, he lived thereafter with a question in his mind. Whether the hand was his or some outside force the question held as question, as insomniac query, query to the gods. Ceaselessly, a difficulty hung in the air, it hung over him. It wasn't to be fingered though. A complication had been deposited that stood as complication. Thought left in suspension; thought a half done sequence; resolution as meaningless as it was impossible. There was fear to go near the complication.

He was asked to baby sit, and agreed to it, the sting of the empty house the thing that was the unknown of unknowns, which he described to himself as the underworld of a marriage.

Duty to his brother demanded he defend her, but, unseen by him, that was his inclination in any case. Always there were the rooms, the best of the rooms Northcroft, where finally a woman's patrols could be, this woman's, at last the planet was in kind, at last the children were grown; and always in these rooms, the early ones the later ones, unconscious of the fact, Craig Mercer' brother watched the woman; not because it was his secret wish to sleep with her; though like most, had his brother not been there, he wouldn't have said no; that wasn't the situation; reserved where his brother was not shy to give an account of himself, deferential to the last of his poor bones, which thankfully wasn't his brother, given that his brother's natural aggressiveness fled as a rule when held in his wife's gaze, Craig Mercer's younger sibling grew to a role of observing, of accepting the preference of others; and once in the role helplessly the muteness strengthened, silent dumbness soon his way. And looking on from the margins, as if an invalid bound to a bed, who was there in front of him one day but this woman his brother had led into the family fold; who anyway, again not really sensed by him at the time, inserted the pause in the mind that compels a person to observe; so that years later, having eventually freed himself from his lifeless place at the side of his brother and taken to his own marriage, marriages, in recalling his former meekness, he found himself revisiting the places where he had been this ghastly cowed figure; and who was to be found in those places but her.

She reappeared to him, led to him this time not by his brother, but by himself. He took on, at once willingly and reluctantly, but somehow inevitably, a new role, that of unspeaking lonely moderator of this one woman. While she lived judgement was the contest she was in, and in the mind of Craig Mercer's brother the contest survives unabated, she judgement's invincible quarry. Judge! Judge her!? Craig Mercer's brother asks that someone show him how you should so much as to start to. He knew her and realises now the boundlessness of that.

Of course, right or wrong in the conclusions he reaches, a man has to judge his colleagues, and without restraint. That is how he casts off deference. She, woman, knew it all. Amongst this isolation a man has with himself is the shout: Be. And that means at some point to remove your heart from others. To live, break the spell of others, and it doesn't matter how it is accomplished. Contempt is strength and so is indifference, insensibility.

Understanding, revelation, as to his ineffable weakness, had reached out to him in the event, her coaching purely. Yes, purely she was a figure of instruction. But it is one thing to receive enlightenment, another to turn the truths to an active philosophy. When necessary the talent never escaped her.

At a particular stage in the story Craig Mercer's brother had direct first-hand experience of it. Facing difficulties in his own marriage he had enquired of his elder sibling if he could have a week's use of the holiday chalet that Craig Mercer kept near to the Welsh coast, just further proof of the Mercer brothers' ineffable history of properties acquired, of properties dispatched so as to advance to the next one.

On this one occasion, Craig Mercer didn't check with his wife, telling his younger kin to go ahead. Within minutes of his arrival at the chalet with his infant child, some three hours spent in the car, Craig Mercer's brother received a telephone call. It was she, the one not consulted. Listening he did not attempt a single word. She had launched into a tirade, the decibels forcing skywards. It had been unending, it had been unceasing scream, it had been inhuman it had been insanity's cousin. Hearing her out, Craig Mercer's bother had been uncomprehending then, he remains uncomprehending to this day. Yes, these were premises belonging to his brother and yes he had wanted to take advantage of their out-of-the-way situation in order to weigh whether his own marriage had a future, and somewhere in the fog of the barrage this consideration seemed definitely implicated as a fuse to the lunatic outpouring, yet still it defies him to explain that telephone call. From where, from what? A man's intelligence was confounded to answer, and ever so.

She had commanded that he take up his child and get out, which he had done, seeking out a hotel in the town. And years after the event, during the weeks following her funeral, a surprise waited for him. A parcel had been left for him in the reception of his offices the size of the trunk he used to go off to boarding school with at the outset of a new term. The delivery man hadn't asked for a signature. Of documentation there wasn't anything. He the driver had set the chest down on the floor, turned, walked out. In the circumstances the delivery received the greatest suspicion from everybody. Once introduced to the contents of the chest, Craig Mercer's brother backed off from an effort to uncover the identity of the person charged to see the shipment effected. Obviously it wasn't Craig Mercer's hand at work. Whoever it was they had had a role of mere agent. His assumption was of a death-bed request. In secret, the end closing in, she had commissioned a friend to perform one last favour. Be it said, the friend needed to delay until after the hospital wasn't of use anymore.

The explanation satisfied him who while she lived had believed himself to be of so much inconsequence for her. Forget it! Whoever it was, it just didn't matter, he cautioned himself. Mightily this was his inclination once he understood what the hefty case held.

Waiting for the end it felt to Craig Mercer's brother that a divergence was made plain. No, a woman wasn't a man. The death of a woman was different. At a man's passing the world straightaway looked round keen to get to hand with the business of replacing him. With a woman's last withdrawal the world knew itself weaker. Somewhere a crack in the structure had just got bigger.

Having peeked inside the chest Craig Mercer's brother went off to a motel and proceeded to tip the contents over the floor. It seemed that behind the curtains of that early buttercup house the underworld of a marriage unfolded from the first day. The trunk released a trove of photographs. Crate, chest, it was, sincerely said, the photographs a good few thousand in number, not a single example amongst them that wasn't a study of the single same person, that didn't attest to the devout concentration and homework this person had extended upon the organization of her shape for each of the shots.

Craig Mercer's marriage had been inaugurated upon his wife's commandment that before he should do anything else this man her husband must agree to the task of committing the twenty-two year old woman to lasting record. Had a house anywhere ever put up the shutters to the world as invincibly as Craig Mercer's in the opening months of the marriage? Walls, nothing to see, nothing to know, but suddenly Craig Mercer's brother knew. Behind the walls had been the young female model, had been the man with the camera. But the man the model had picked on to be the man with the camera was her husband who remained oblivious of the hard use she would make of him until they reached the house designated for their life together.

He had had to learn how to do this. But the lenses as eyes were to one end exclusively. Her! He would sleep beside the woman, he would rise to a form of slavery at her feet. Meals would be forgotten, a house would be plundered as bare out stage and backdrop. Sofas, armchairs, beds, straight-back chairs, kitchen stools, tables, doorways, staircase, stairs so much the regulation flight of a regulation hallway in a regulation house, everything was co-opted as crutch to her posing.

The house was soon sweltering immersion, immersion to the labour that had been set. Day long she had posed and perhaps sometimes night long too, the changing choreography of arms, legs, head, shoulders like a crunching of numbers. And so had been the endless swapping of dress. The photographs launched through the whole landscape of a woman's wrapping of her body, should this dare to pursue the minimal, frank insight of the body, should this go to the fully laden, some gown proper to a ball. But whether or not two years or so before she had done voluntary duty as her college's life model, the expression on her face suggesting it wasn't anything more than what a person had to do, not one of the cache of photographs delivered so mysteriously to Craig Mercer's brother some twenty years following the period when they were taken, represented a composition of her naked.

Yet, somewhat strange in the understanding, given what was occurring on the interior of the house, it is when focusing on this phase the revelation unfolds of a definite couple encamped behind the first set of walls Craig Mercer had title to. Without hesitation the verdict is that two they were during those months, two meaning to be two, two flush with the seal of two.

And so much that at every part of the house, at every part of the day; the joined when she arranged herself in front of him; the joined still through the pauses when she went off to change her clothes; no less when he was the one creeping off, his first cell of shame in the marriage, these vapid holes where he was frozen out, the dark room he had fashioned from the space beneath the stairs, not any aspect of this toil, of the whole business of photography, of the least interest to him.

But did that matter, because two they were then; in his idolization of the face he was coaxing to life under the surface of the solutions in the trays; in his feeling of being obliterated by this obsession of hers; in his understanding that the photographs he was developing hadn't felicity, joy, just a dread strain, some nameless exertion after a goal only she knew and knowing didn't begin to know.

And bound just as much as she waited for him to bring the prints out to her; bound as, uselessly, he was left to watch her pore through them, her gaze for her own image like some fight to the death; bound equally in his wonder at her and this nameless rite which had become the swearing in of a marriage

And weren't they two still at sunset, after she had called a stop for the day, he numb with the understanding that the patterns she followed once they were released from the terrible business for another day, from nowhere took him as focus.

And the lock about two people persisted when later alone he lay on the bed of the first-floor room, a built-in mahogany wardrobe running parallel with the bed at the right with inset mirrors the full height of the doors, and in perfect passivity returned to what had occurred not in the morning or that afternoon but in the minutes that were still damp about him, the minutes that hadn't yet departed the space beside him, that were there still to nudge, and which he was frightened to do out of the sudden enormous compassion for himself that came over him at his good fortune just to have met this woman.

Left to himself in the bedroom, the act without description again put away, sitting up languidly against the pillows, seeing outside the window the neighbourhood's orchards of antennae-struck rooftops, in this interlude, over and over, he knew minutely of a bliss of surfeit.

In these minutes, helplessly, all of it just fell back through his mind.

How at day's end she suddenly could break out in awareness of the two they were then and what she had for this man she was with. How at dusk he was returned to the person he had married. How after the feral onslaught of another of these days of the camera, invariably she had a keenness to bathe. How she liked to delve amongst her bottles in the choosing of which salts to intoxicate the water with, to coax the water with, the better to experience the dew in the water, the better to experience the water weeping, her flesh weeping in the long lucid second of contact.

How emerging from the bathroom, the towel long and enveloping, she would flick the buried wound of a smile, gone even as it formed, but in the memory of it running out to the sort of spasm in time that will see a sailing dingy tip crazily then right itself, which in fact might too have been the smile. But wasn't the smile as well a sort of ashes, aglow yet, which glimmer in the context of a woman could never go out properly, vivid as it was of tenderness, expectancy, disenchantment, repentance, dismissal, sacrifice, duty, conceit, and on. Yes, this pain for a thing a woman needs to express before ever the action is begun.

How then turning away she would head straight for the bed, the step sharp and decisive but with this other face to it which was stealth. How throwing herself forward at the edge of the bed, a figure sheathed to the armpits, she would metamorphose into this turtle as she scrambled across to the side of the bed in the sway of the wardrobe with its leagues of reflective glass.

How at this junction she would ignore the panels of glass. How it was then that while stretched out full length on her back, to the current of arm and leg an absorbing lifelessness, all the grace and remoteness of Mary in this figure of a woman shrouded in a long white towel, awful chasteness to the shape of a person precisely where the shape reeked of human impurity, she would without stirring summon about herself some indefinable cubicle of protection, not an actual wall anywhere beyond the towel.

How daring to his place his hand on her, he was kept at a terrible distance, informed that it was mere radiance he was caressing, a radiance wrought of her but still a parody of the reality of a person he was in search of, that he bled to reach, that he yearned for frankly and unreservedly.

Her radiance and with it at this stage of things her controlled indifference; how everything would be in suspension now because it was the timing that mattered, and, as it has been indicated, it was timing she had a feel for, in this situation a perfect tension for. Yes, how it was for her to decide when, how it was for her to choose. And how it was, in the goodness of time, lifting herself up slightly, that her arm jerked, that with this action the towel came out, was sent off somewhere, finishing you supposed on the floor, or thereabouts.

How, without her doing anything more, all this living archness of woman suddenly burst from her; she lay, she was nude, she was a sphinx from all the ages in the knowledge of what she was showing, up there somewhere beneath the brow small round eyes deathly quiet, deathly still, a stillness spread through with the opera of her breasts, the orbs motionless too, waiting like she was waiting,

How a lasting dawn fastened to the room with the weight of this riotous breaking out of one woman's reservoirs of beauty, and she yet a step or two back from that dawn, as it came, as it went on, crescendo to crescendo; even if later, years later, he didn't see that she was ever like this with the stable girls, for then surely it was her who was the supplicant.

How the instant he came off her she would turn on to her side to face the wide wardrobe with its minions of mirrors; yes, how, his furores paid out, without further ado her mind in a second was somewhere else, and so shatteringly fast you realized all the time she had been fully conscious of the shelter of the looking glass waiting. And once she found herself he was nowhere, simply meaningless, regardless that there he lay, the whole surfeited length of him, there right up against her back, his lips pressed to her shoulder as if in prayer.

That she lived!

How in these seconds, cold to his presence, she sought out her image with the largest quietest eyes she brought to anything. How in these seconds everything of herself converged to observation of herself, the silence in the room going on, and inside that silence the silence of it, of this her confession, her absolution, her everlasting imploration of self, her everlasting devotions to self.

How in these seconds he knew to his soul his invisibility. How to his immense regret nevertheless she would eventually lever herself off the bed, gather up the towel so as to head off into the good-proportioned room, her leaving like a tearing of his flesh, in search of the lone refrigerator-size mirror housed on a far wall.

How reaching this mirror, the towel around her by now, she spread the towel out until it made these wings extending off her back to each side. How, so upright, so bare, she then just went to gazing anew; how then it was just nothing but the body of a woman the eyes of a woman; how under the pressure of her own naked form came about a concentration drowning out the world; how the bed in the room turned as old in its meaning as some event from the long past, though to Craig Mercer's own eyes retaining enough relevance for him to see the thing that had occurred upon it only this minute as firing anew this person who had slanted her way to the far side of the room like some raw picking from the natural world, whatever the air of remorse about her.

And how once arrived at the object in the room she was intent on she allowed this moment of her standing alone and naked at the mirror endure. How, the eyes she stared with a font of loving gazing, a sheer gravity of moment would spread out in the room that had Craig Mercer, not a reflective man, turning from the devout busyness of the world, this brewery the street was, to listen to echo, to listen to force fields, energies not anything to do with a man, and as remote, intangible and opaque to understanding as the undertows of the ocean depths.

Years and years after her passing it was that Craig Mercer had started to bear witness to his brother, though in the telling leaving his brother with a poignant sense that a human being was lowering out of sight of the imagination of the man she had made a family with, a man who, yes, had in time consented to a new union.

And finally sifting through the photographs that had come into his possession in the weeks succeeding her funeral, which prior to himself he was convinced had only ever been viewed by three people, the woman, her husband and the person who had — at her death-bed entreaty presumably — gone to the trouble to deposit them with him, Craig Mercer's brother discovered a sequence that must have come about at the finish of the episode of the photography, an episode initiating a marriage. In these images she was captured in dark trousers and white masculine shirt, her hair cropped short, almost savagely so.

Years and years down the road this was how she made an entrance one day to the building representing Craig Mercer's offices. Nor was it a case of a lady calling at her husband's place of work whilst she happened to be in town for the day. In this way she had of just overriding the world and everyone in it, she was presenting herself as the company's newest employee, and certainly not to be classed with the junior staff. Least of all was it to be an unpaid position.

Common sense said that Craig Mercer should have got this past his American masters before he had given in to her. But it had been put to him as her spending agendas were put to him. He might have imagined he was sitting in judgement on her newest determination for her life, that the back and forth of his meditation on the matter had meaning, that he was entitled to believe himself the demonstrable authority that would decide the issue. In fact his contemplations, whatever their seriousness to him, were little more than pantomime.

He was to have a new personal assistant and he had better get used to the idea.

But Craig Mercer was not running his own company, he was the local officer, if the most senior, of an international organization. This was an intelligent woman; could she have been so blind to the dangers of her actions for her husband, and therefore for her, and worse, for the whole family?

He had persuaded the Americans of the benefits of moving the offices of their United Kingdom subsidiary out of the city. It was a constellation of market towns ringing the city, precisely her origins; in fact though the particular town enshrining her beginnings didn't receive a moment's consideration from him as he selected amongst the group. It was about the greyest, drabbest of them anyway. Another boasted the region's iconic cathedral, this great secreted imbalanced kernel to a town, enthroned against the immediate buildings circling it like a mounded precious stone in its setting. At a distance from the town its three spires reached proud of the lines of roofs to fabulous effect. Yet finding oneself on foot in the streets it became the town's great secret. It couldn't be suspected of existing until a person fell over the short road at whose end was situated the cathedral close.

Hadn't Craig Mercer been a cathedral school boy, of perfectly cherubic face? What a solid flock of venerably styled houses made up the close and wedged between the residences of the bishops and deacons were the two buildings, one at each end of the close, constituting the preparatory school he had attended. The second of the buildings had in times past been the bishop's palace. If once in service as amongst other things, dungeons, that section of the building existing below ground level could for a school's young population establish itself as a universe its own.

The boarding school boys had their locker rooms down there. In the underground passages at different times of the day the boys cued up in perennial fashion. Leading off the passages were all sorts of rooms, bays, the ceilings not letting you off a moment in their curving nearness. In these areas the fresh-faced and believing, Craig Mercer with them, learnt to box. To a man possessed of white hands frail-looking like lace, these little shapes found where the arms finished, still to form really, got stuffed down into something from the shelves of an armoury. In the subterranean world of a bishop's palace, in buried compartments like cannon siloes, the decidedly mannered boys boxed hard with each other, they bloodied each other, the battling moreover forcing some of the young to tears, this tender despairing figure in impeccable vest suddenly halting at the centre spot of the makeshift ring in a rebellion of saints, his arms dropping to his side like weights, his lips welling at the ridiculousness, the crazy impossibility, of what was being asked of him, the red engulfing his eyes translating as utter abject surrender in the face of the miserable hopeless thing which was a boy's life.

Out on a walk in the town environs a band of twenty of this superior sort of child would turn and flee meeting face on down a narrow path just one of the town's common born youths.

On the floors above the palace's fighting rings were areas ready-made to do duty as dormitories. Outside the windows of the dorms, as if set up on chocks at the centre-patch of the arena that was the stately close, its surface pitted, gnarled, callused, was this gargantuan moth-balled submarine, an overarching colossus as immovable as time. It had its crews too, the young school members a part of them, the uniform for the job involving fully-fledged skirts.

The open paved space stretched before the cathedral was like a Roman way, invested with a gaze to outer bounds of such thrust and appetite and enquiry it didn't just fling back gates, walls, it sent them spinning. The town itself just couldn't rise to eyes like this, the stodgy, roofed-in stalls that broke out at the town centre on market day the image of the town's natural impulses.

All towns have crime-rates, even saintly ones, and there's a terrible inward-directedness to crime rates as there's a terrible inward-directedness to some provincial towns. The walls are not to go past but in the comforting horizons they erect to be treated as governance, as the faithful prescriptive article of what is and of what may be. And behind such walls the days, the years, faithfully they link up, faithfully are they put away.

At the end of each summer term it was a practice of the cathedral school to arrange a cricket match between the principal school eleven and the fathers of the boys concerned. For Craig Mercer and his own father the match in this series that had represented the closing act not just of another summer term but of the years of Craig Mercer's entire stay at this particular school had been little short of a disaster. One of the decisions of the captain of the father's side was to unload onto Craig Mercer's father the not inconsiderable responsibilities, and dangers, of cover-point, the elders, the toss in their favour, having elected to take to the field.

Perhaps the relative proximity of the father to the crease had affected the son. In any case, it had been a decidedly self-conscious young individual Craig Mercer's father had witnessed arrive at the stumps and go to readying himself. At the very first delivery Craig Mercer had launched himself forward bereft of the most minimal caution, the swing of the bat as huge as it was aberrant. Nonetheless, the boy's eye had been good, bat centring on ball to perfection. Something had left the bat, this something nothing short of a missile, its velocity to terrible to belong to the world, the deadly piece starting at waist height and not veering a millimetre up or down as it streaked through the air, the passage something like an extended detonation never captured by the human eyes at any single point only as a flashing compilation of many points.

What could the poor fool at cover-point have known beyond the fact that he was the person in the firing line? Perhaps the poor fool who was Craig Mercer's father hadn't even known that. In his human sources annulled of anything but base instinct he had stuck his arm sharply out, the action belonging to him, not belonging to him.

The hand of a man spread the ball had gone home as death comes in a war, no bullet straighter or faster at the fateful moment of impact. It was as if at the second of collision he had been divorced from his hand, but hand it was, someone's anyway, and it did its work, the fingers closing around the object sweetly, rapidly, the motion as organized and sure as a robot will bring off.

A look of mild surprise had entered the face of the man. With the force of the impact Craig Mercer's father should have been pushed back on his feet. Instead there had been not a flicker, the figure of a man rigid and holding, the right arm jutting at ninety degrees rod-firm, the large hand never more vividly large, its clutch on the ball larger.

For long seconds that is how he had remained, frozen like a stone statue. The spectators at the boundary hadn't moved a muscle. A hush like mourning had gripped a sports field. Finally the young one had turned from the crease, beginning the bitter trail back to the pavilion, a child's head sunk like a circus clown's. At his place in the field, a man in the middle period of his life had hardly dared bring himself to watch, crammed as he was by the poignancy of his son's walk back, crammed by the protracted time it had taken. Out first ball! Damnation on the father! Find him one of the dungeons in the old palace. Lose the key!

In the event Craig Mercer, his father very much still alive, was to introduce a portion of the wider planet to this one stifling, dully staid, ritual-fast market town, a lead in its look and ways so much the concomitant of these narrow spots off in land's deep interior.

The National Westminster Bank had abruptly put their building of time-honoured presence, of time-honoured architecture, up for auction. Empowered by the Americans to bid for it, Craig Mercer attended the sale knowing he would be the victor. Of course, in arguing his case with his American principals as to the good sense of vacating the city it had never evaded his meditations that the market town lay hardly more than a mile from the village that he and his family were becoming established in. Taking time out from the village, the town was on any day his wife's first port of call, though in her adherence to the streets and its shops, he didn't mislead himself into imagining her visits implied even a vague consciousness of the connection the town had to his early story.

Surely he was right. She did her casual shopping there. A woman had to pin some place down for this. She was demanding with the criteria to be met, but not altogether so. She didn't demand the capital. And suddenly, the move from the city complete, inside one of the most authoritative buildings in the town was this man she had taken as her husband. But he didn't sit there in isolation. Present around him was the official world he ruled over.

For years the Americans in the main had been willing to leave Craig Mercer to his own devices, satisfied that persistent oversight wasn't necessary in his case, even a suggestion in the air that the faraway chiefs couldn't be bothered with England, whether or not their presence in the country was long established. For years no one had visited from the organization's base on the other side of the Atlantic. Always Craig Mercer had journeyed to America to make his reports. But hardly had he got to his new offices away from the city than he was put on notice to expect the arrival of a delegation from the U.S.A. some four months hence. At last his principals' interest was piqued. They were keen to inspect the building they had acquired. Craig Mercer's description of it had been telling; enough that it was the reason that had inspired their go ahead for the purchase.

Once apprised of the coming of the Americans did she know fear? Did she sense mortal danger? By her actions to avert the danger wasn't it true she multiplied no end this peril to her husband that with her intelligence she had intercepted, becoming herself amongst the most significant agents of Craig Mercer's drawn out dislodging from his privileged position, which crisis came to a head in the months after her funeral, instigating for Craig Mercer the start of another protracted crisis, that with his son?

Historic the building might have been but it was rundown. She elected herself as the person best qualified to bring it to an order that would please the Americans, for as she argued to herself with impeccable judgement, if in the event they weren't satisfied by the investment her husband had pushed them to enter on it might follow that their marvellous trust in her husband might take one of those blows the deadliness of which isn't apparent at first. Where a man pays your wage, should you raise him to some definite excitement, but then disappoint him in his hopes, thereafter the shade on his heart, the sense of betrayal, will wear your face.

But even possessed of this argument that it was necessary for her to insert herself into her husband's offices for his own safety and the family's, how could she have resisted anyway. It was all coming to her and she wasn't about to leave out the last part. Pulled by dark covetousness, daily she went to war with the marriage, yet daily she was guided by it like nothing else. Craving of life experiences like she craved was a pivot that minute by minute turned her inside out, and that is how she proceeded from one day to the next.

What had come first was the village and the florid existence she was soon making for herself there, and the nearby town was quickly the complement to the existence; so with her husband's seat of power all of a sudden at the heart of the town, literally, the woman seen in the last of the photographs Craig Mercer had devoted himself to at the outset of their marriage reappeared with a vengeance. There was somewhere, precisely, where this woman could be, and of course at some stage she had to be.

Years before she had put on a business get-up for him to capture her like that in print, now years later she adopted the same attire to head straight for him who in their life together in the village she could with her conduct send against a wall of insanity.

A building that was amongst the town's most significant markers, Craig Mercer one of the town's monarchs if for no other reason than the building he was king over, she had a new cause, a new heart's wish. And then, of course, always there was this tension she occupied, lived out, of craving a stage for herself that went beyond her roots, though always failing to succeed to the courage for those bounds. What better substitute could there have been? She could play out the drama of the great wide world without taking a step away from the man she clung to, from the town she clung to; so long of course as she got herself a role, a place inside the building entirely perceivable as a sampling of the citadels of power laid at her feet.

The staircase that led to the first floor landing was broad like a boulevard. Beneath the carpet the rungs were concave from wear. Time, history, resides in some staircases, far beyond what any wall will print on the mind.

But it wasn't the staircase that rushed to her. It was the general spaces of the three floors. Say it again: on her legs, visibly, tangibly, the limbs powering down, she was a martial force. The stride she had, it beat a tattoo.

One force meeting another because the building itself up there at the head of the road was the road's unequivocal ox. The four outside walls bore this as their stamp like little else. And didn't they, in the light of the coming arrival of the Americans, shout to be seen to as much as the interior of the building, across their white colour an ancient tarnish too much the gutter's befouling, abstract dribbles of dark staining descending from the corners of every one of the ornate window ledges.

The horses didn't go with her into the building. This place in the town, this one building, it was a woman in her other ramifications, her other complicities, her other planets. The horses, even as mere notion, weren't anywhere.

There appeared the office professional, the bureaucrat of perfect competence, and proud in it. Beholding the efficiency, the accomplishment forming to her effortlessly, like snow breaks out, it left sadness, because a comparable effectiveness never quite came to her in her life with the horses, though she strained for it, and didn't she? Visibly over time she wore the blighted skin the sun wreaks on man. But the absolute exertion she put into the horses told on her no less. Yes, too much of existence she met without the mention of tenderness; by that engrossment, tyranny, somehow she wasn't treated tenderly, not in body, not you have to think in soul.

In time there arose the idea that the surface marking on the body resounded to a significant degree as a cost forged by the relentlessness occurring on the inside. Was the idea so wrong? Quite simply, this was the relentless woman. Without mercy for herself in advance of the damage her hard dimensions inflicted on others, which they did.

The dual assault had to be. It could not have been otherwise. In any case, the years going on forests of stress lines lurked. She couldn't hold them off. Endlessly, she drove herself like an engine.

Once the first-floor landing in the building was attained the door to her husband's office lay off to the right. In her vixen business attire she arrived in the building a galvanized figure. Parallel with the management duties she took on herself the responsibility of a complete reworking of Craig Mercer's office. If the Americans had forgotten who it was who had charge of their affairs in the United Kingdom, his office would introduce him to them in significant terms.

This interior design job she gave herself in consort with her administrative duties wouldn't be easy since to accomplish the project it would be necessary to work around her husband, and in action in the office Craig Mercer was a tireless figure of combat. He knew not how to be still. Eight or so houses this couple took up station in while she lived and a sofa in the lounge finally attained in the evening Craig Mercer did at last quieten, bringing one leg up to hook it beneath the other. Only under pressure to hold a formal meeting did he ever close the door to his office. But as to the general flow of the day it was his management style to stay visible to those who served him, the basis of his office door not a barred way but a public way. It could result in his being casually hailed from the entrance to the room, even by the most junior of the staff, like some ship's lookout.

At his desk down at the opposite end of the room from the entrance, it was likely he would answer the queries of the figure arrived in the doorway without lifting his head from the paper he was studying. Opening inwards the actual door to the room passed the hours lying flush with the outside wall beyond which was a central street of shops and cafeterias, a hair-dressing salon the first thing seen from the window at this part of the office.

The vantage point permitted a detailed view of the many photographs of models the salon had hung on one side of their premises. Curiously, the large photograph that was first in the line represented a composition of one of the young women working on the ground floor of Craig Mercer's building who happened to be a frequent customer of the salon, and whose portrait the salon had been keen to make use of in a promotional context for the very reason that she was in possession of a face of enchanting beauty. Even fifteen years before Gillian Mercer couldn't have claimed fairness like this. Of the town's girls that Craig Mercer employed this young woman's looks just went to something else. But at some level of personality this seemed to leave her anxious, even frightened, for all that the photograph of her hoisted up in the salon stared at you undaunted in its place alongside images of faces with a professional claim to beauty, these young women established as models down in London, somewhere Craig Mercer would come to knowledge of in that last lunge for a cure to his wife's cancer. He knew it of course from his business existence, but entering a place to save a person's life, the buildings, the streets, they changed around in their essence, their colours.

The photograph of that office girl of his that the salon had arranged was the starkest evidence that horizons were open to her that would have the town and its works simply a forgotten spot in the hinterland, born into but jettisoned as swiftly as one could. And the evidence must have haunted her, having this understanding of herself, like coals on her inside, that she would never leave the area, this one market town, or at least what it stood for, identifiably the actual future she would accept and give herself to.

Craig Mercer's desk, off in the other direction in the presidential room, and which she his wife and newest employee soon had exchanged for something far grander, lay angled slightly between two windows. The end wall housing one of the windows was situated at the back of the desk, the other inset into the long side wall of the room. It was this side window that looked out onto the intersection that the building dominated, a significant free area over the way because the girl's day school facing Craig Mercer's building, brown woollen skirts and blouses, yellow ties at the collars, was set well back from where the cars and pedestrians passed along.

Should they choose to make a left turn at the intersection the cars followed the frontage of the building looped with the shops, the building's main entrance here. It was a left turn that was forced on the visitor to the building arriving on foot once he had passed beneath the great arch of the street entry. At night formidable black-painted wrought-iron gates sealed the street entryway. Taking a step off the street brought a person into a sheer-walled alcove of broad squares of brown-tinged stone, as single pieces rectangles with a dimension on a par with the mighty panels of charcoal slate establishing the roof of the building.

Completing the bound off the sidewalk it was one more left turn that was asked for. The manoeuver led the visitor through a glass door and on down a short passageway, the outside wall at his left shoulder characterised by a line of large windows above head height. Within ten further paces he was confronted by the building's reception desk, but the presence of the receptionist herself had to be taken on trust because she was concealed by a gargantuan switch-board that must have been a relic of the Second World War. Somehow it told of those sleepless operations rooms in which the bombing raids of legend had been launched. And in a way so did the girls that Craig Mercer set to work at the desks on the ground floor of the building, all of these stations visible to the visitor once he or she had reached the receptionist's own place, a waist high wall at the right providing a unobstructed view of an expansive area that was like a sort of pit, a plethora of stubby desks as if afloat across the hollow.

So it was these girls who in their dress and faces, though strangely excluding the girl adorning the wall of the hair-dressers salon, harked back somehow to a type of Anglo-Saxon young woman that libraries of black and white photographs have documented for posterity, a tribe of doughty twenty-year olds who so significantly got to their womanhood in wartime. Gillian Mercer herself, in her days in the office, in addition to the black trousers, she likewise would wear these waging robust martial-tinged skirts that while extolling the woman as straight-out presence were at pains also to describe the no-nonsense service she was about.

Throughout the day all of these people followed each other in standing in the ever yawning, ever encouraging, ever bidding, entrance to Craig Mercer's office. And standing took their medicine. His head wasn't always lowered. Not a bit. And don't think that the figure in the doorway was any wishing well. It was the rack he was on with his responsibilities. At a distance of some twenty-five feet he directed, ordered, urged, cajoled, despaired, denounced, denigrated, pleaded, shot lethal looks, blackened names, pronounced himself blameless, threw fits. At turns, he let fly, whatever the sex of the person in front of him. And it happened on more days than was comfortable in the assessment. But don't those who work for a man resolve to shake off the bad, knowing themselves, fervently, to be God's witness to the real human being behind the desk. The emotional injuries of the workplace can't detract from the suspicion that in one aspect what a man asks for from another is to be pierced by something, revelation, bliss, that will leave him ready to walk through fire on the other's behalf. Sanity is the leader, so believe you must.

In any case the staff, they knew. Their man, he was tension, she the merciless one, breath hot, just born again in his poor ear. She upended his last redoubt. But hadn't he of his own free will elected to abandon the city.

At his desk Craig Mercer went to chanting in one of the two fully-formed voices he realised in his marriage, each coming to him out at the peripheries of the thing that was the union between two people, somewhere outside of the orbit of the rooms and houses he actually inhabited with his wife.

The first of the voices, heard where he had his work, and so indelibly in time a fixture of these places, and indeed to be taken as that sound which is the business executive heaving under the strain, was indeed a chant.

To get to the heart of this chant it is necessary to draw attention to the word I as it is manifested in English. Those references a man makes to his country that flow from his identification with it demand that he defer to his place in the crowd. He is simply one of many and knows himself as such. Of course, he will say 'I' am American or 'I' am English, but after that it is a matter of 'our' rivers capture the eye, or 'we' will succeed in the coming war.

And in these contexts, as much as the next man, Craig Mercer was all modesty; the 'we' issuing from his lips couldn't be faulted. It was so properly a matter of reflex, the evident enthusiasm in the sound no less convincing than could be captured from the efforts of his neighbour, accepting that a man would sound somewhat absurd were he not to fall in line. My rivers! Hardly!

In some directions the language reaching his tongue followed all normal precedents, bearing witness to a person admirably in touch with his communal insignificance. But when it came to the world he ruled over, when the men he was directing were his men, the verbal routine became of another cast altogether. Somewhere this brave 'we' died without trace. It became impossible for him to refer to the accomplishments or activities of the organization he was captain of without concentrating the whole edifice of the organization into what has been described as the most concentrated word in any language, the English term I. Whatever the newest achievement of the organization, all had to acknowledge that from birth as a bare idea through to the point of realization as product or surpassing strategy, there had been but one all-encompassing architect, the single same hand pulling at every oar. And how did one understand it? Because all one needed to do was resort to the power of one's hearing. Almost every statement escaping his lips in connection with the company and its accomplishments was liable to carry from an identical beginning: the word I.

There were days in the office when there was hardly an utterance of his that wasn't conceived in the single same manner. Indeed, with the devilish readiness of this the most compulsive of all words to ensnare and intoxicate a man, it has to be asked whether the inevitable seduction was ever so complete as in his own case.

The second full-blown voice he blossomed to, reaped sanction for, in his marriage opened off the existence of his son. In the office, the avowal of himself that he found in the word I, outside the office, outside the houses, the avowal that was his son's name. From a certain stage, the boy blossoming, any chance to crow about his son he started in before you could blink. In fact he never waited for the invitation; whatever the company the word flooded from him. The noise seemed a taunt against the world. The noise put the world on notice; purely that the human like wasn't on offer at another place across the globe.

Really the second voice was the telling of a story: that a son existed, that the son was his. And isn't the story heard wherever a conversation is struck up with a man. This thing that goes for a man: the life hurtles on but the way of speech, its content, is set in stone. The dawns too numerous to count what you hear from a man is a given number of exhortations. It's a rare day the impersonal features. Too much does a man come to be but to complete the one boast, though of course the revelation must wait on the appearance of the son before it is proven beyond all question;

But Craig Mercer you couldn't look at without bringing his wife into it. The second of the voices he achieved, no less than the first in fact, had to be accepted also as a cry of bitterness at the endless side-lining he suffered at the hands of his wife and therefore the world. Never more was the son-god to be seen as certified angel of need; pure gold, an entrance coming to the aid of the man.

Two voices, and this the second, plaintive as the first, grew from the very real shouting that Craig Mercer engaged in in racing up and down the touchlines of various sports-fields. He cheered on like this was the reason for existence. He cheered on and couldn't stop wherever he was, a true voice realised at last, and as this one the splinter took shape.

Craig Mercer's young male offspring was a player. Football resonated as amongst the strongest of the games; tennis was another at the public school. That said it's not to be excluded that at fourteen Craig Mercer's boy showed himself to be seriously incomplete in his footballing proficiency. He was largely numb to the game unless the ball was there to feint with, to put the force to. He was this lost abject figure when the ball lay not with him; without instinct for the simple green of a football pitch, its yawning avenues; blind to the ability to read a match; was devoid of the feeling to roam, to glide like a shark, to breast space like a swallow; couldn't wing things in anticipation, in sure knowledge; just without the insight to discern the spot to be for the game to come to him; without the gut instinct for the moving map of a game; hollow to the vision to find his own team inside the map.

He was the starkest evidence that a person is born to this sport clean out. There were boys on his school team who when the ball was with others were imperious masters of space. They could have been conquistadors on horseback eyeing the natives with contempt. They loved the space they loved the thing in them that told them how to garner the space for the greatest profit. They loved being a lone figure free on a park, the marvel being that in this free running a team got its centre.

To be a functioning part in the game Craig Mercer's boy needed the bright object fixed to the toecaps of his boots, and what he did then hardly varied. He took off hard he took off straight, direct at the nearest player on the opposing side, the test to go round him with a brilliant swerve of the body, the test to floor the youth with the manoeuvre. If he succeeded, then at last he would lift his head. His vision appeared locked to the ten yards in front of him.

Later, with the undying help of his father, he became the most professional, skilled and secure of airline pilots, his touch for machine, for the great park which is the ether, God sent. The cockpit of a jet is the open, the boundless. The cockpit of a jet is man supreme. But by then she had gone.

The village, the town, Craig Mercer's office building in the town, the boy's public school, it was a clique of places, all near to each other. It was the Mercers' very personal circuit. Had the boy been able to see into his father's offices on an average day he perhaps wouldn't have recognized his mother, for finding herself framed by that tellingly dethroned space which was Craig Mercer's office door, she was no different in her responses to any; not to ranking executive, to faint-hearted lackey, doing just as they did, speeding off in a moment to carry out the instructions of the man the Americans relied on in the United Kingdom.

Nor was it any different when later she made this demand of him that he provide her with an apartment in the town in order that at five o' clock she needn't if she chose return to the house, bungalow, Evinrude, but go to a separate existence; and at the entrance of which apartment one day later on still, Northcroft now the official family base, her adolescent son stood in fury to block the way of the newest of her man friends. But who in fact wasn't new at all but someone returned from her past that originally she had gone with prior to her first meeting with Craig Mercer.

And then do not forget the general staff in the building in the town, her husband's staff, for there too she took lovers. For some of the women of her social circles her perennial waywardness became a model of behaviour to absorb and take to as what might be, even as what should be, and the more so did it after she had gone. But practised by others such conduct became just cheap, the height of tawdriness. It can only be said that as women they just didn't have what she had. That anyway is how Craig Mercer's brother describes it to himself, searching to get to grips with the illumination she was impacted with: the grace of woman, as silhouette, as motion. At a certain pitch it's a grace that excuses. She descended, almost beyond description, but then she appeared in a room, and in that coming could be riveting. Unconscionable often, masses of contact with her having her as just plain ordinary, then from nowhere the spur inside one to remember her, to know something: that no mistake she went forward categorically as one unto herself, the very demons profounder.

It happened that one day, there within the family, what was left of it, that Craig Mercer's brother missed her. Going back in his mind, it happened that a simple recognition broke over him, that where she came on any day, this was the family. That as a woman, in her best moments – and yes, wildness, and explicit – too true there streamed off her this extraordinary magnification, too true there appeared something eternal about her. The fever of woman: pigments like dew where the body is, a sentence of torment where the mind dwells. Be it ten million of the earth's female kind passing in front of you not at any point, critically, is it to be identified. Then, without warning, the sky opens, the one comes. But she, Gillian Mercer, could take another woman down, the sharpest, singly mercurial talons in the pen.

So it was on her arrival in the substantial noble epoch-washed town landmark of a building that Craig Mercer was invited to sit by and heed the transformation of his office, which after all had once been home to a high officer of one of the land's powerhouse clearing banks. So it was that by the triumph of her reworking of the office she sealed more comprehensively than ever the immense delusion that three people had been helplessly succumbing to year following year, this three that was herself, her son and her husband, and which is to be understood as the hallucination that no one stood behind Craig Mercer, that he answered to no one, that in fact he was entirely his own man, that the business enterprise he went to each day to direct and govern was nothing so much as his.

With the impending visit of the Americans, their first for who knew how long, Craig Mercer convincing them of the opportuneness of making a move for the old bank hub, she saw the need to act. But the foreign owners of the company having seemingly ignored their United Kingdom offshoot for years, the existence the Mercers were in fact living in England amazingly no longer took them into account. Ostensibly inserting herself into the building to protect her husband and her family, the very people she went in fear of she at the same time treated as not existing. And to attempt to answer the question of why, intelligent as she was, she appeared blind to the obvious terrible impertinence of her presence in the building in the eyes of the owners of the company, all that can be put up is the great fantasy that one family had adopted.

But, of course, blind she so definitely would be because if she wanted something, truly wanted it, the desire was silence of all else. And once Craig Mercer had hold of this building in the town, one of the town's most naturally imposing, she was going to get into it, close to the man, under the aegis of the man, who time and again in their personal life together she left then went back to.

Come the Americans did. She had her own office in the building, she was taking the company's money over and above the salary her husband was paid. And Craig Mercer had said not a word to them. Nothing showed immediately; they were quite content with the building when they were confronted with it; and it would be some years before they actually dispensed with Craig Mercer. But being brought face to face with her in the place where blamelessly they didn't anticipate finding her their trust in Craig Mercer, solid before, was lethally compromised.

But the one in whom the delusion of the American's non-existence waged strongest was her son, their son. From a certain day in time the emerging individual saw the office that she his mother refashioned so majestically as his destiny. Control of this enterprise that was the underpinning of one of the nation's families in time would pass to him. From that would grow his life. And face to face alone with his father at Northcroft in the weeks after her incarceration, that was when the letter arrived, the letter ending Craig Mercer's employment with the mighty American corporation.

It was to be that while she lived she would redo Craig Mercer's office once more, shortly before the day when, in the great action of departing for all time, she made her exit for Timothy Faragher. All these roads people take to to leave behind a life when in actual fact this not what these roads are at all. Craig Mercer was left staring in consternation at the enormous colour print she had had installed above the mock fireplace, a photograph depicting a helmeted black mineworker at the rock-face of a South African gold mine, at a total loss to comprehend her thinking in this choice of picture for his office. But before he could question her she had already absconded, setting her car along the road south.

And when she returned it didn't occur to him to ask, nor was it about to. She had been experiencing difficulty in getting her words out, through and past her lips. She would have the words in view, she would gird herself in great anguished breaths to form them in sound, but the effort increasingly produced nothing. The diagnosis had been swift: brain cancer. Not delaying, Craig Mercer telephoned his brother, having chosen him to be the outlet by which the world would be informed.

And afterwards at Northcroft, because it needed only nine months, had been two people, a man and his son of eighteen. Or was it seventeen? Anyway Northcroft had quickly spun to a house of inquisition, Craig Mercer's son becoming possessed, the man on trial Craig Mercer himself. The younger man started to go days when he lost kindness for his father. Alone together, head to head in an empty mansion, the thankless authoritarian demeanours the junior of the two assumed in his inconsolableness dished out one brutality after another in the direction of the man he was forced to stare at. Any promise there may have been that the long mauling of Craig Mercer was due to end didn't last a day. Let it be said that the brutality for a seventeen year old was the vagabond anger that in waves he wept with helpless as a goat on a chain.

It was at about this point that the word that was Craig Mercer's son's name began to die on Craig Mercer's lips, but he didn't abandon the word, it held fast to his soul, and along with the great flying deeds that his son went on to out of the need to discover a career for himself when as in his own mind the promised heir to his father he had always taken the career for granted, continued to inform Craig Mercer as to his own qualities and strengths as a man, never failed to act as a buttress of his self-worth, persisted simply to instruct him as to who he was, this aging man whose wife was taken from him when she was forty-two years old.

Getting back to Northcroft from the church Craig Mercer found himself journeying duty-bound between various small groups on the inside of the house, and, unlike his brother, was unaware of the drama of the yard beyond the kitchen window, of how falling foul of the space one then another of those who had been at the church turned to these wretched slack-limbed facsimiles of a human being, each of them in turn compelled to send their drained eyes off past the tall open-sided barn and away to the vacant fields, yet seeing none of it, just the image of this singular woman in riding breeches standing with her hand held out, one of her thoroughbreds arched down at the ration of straw lying in her lax grip, its tender muzzle suckling her palm.

CPSIA information can be obtained
at www.ICGtesting.com
Printed in the USA
LVOW12s1145200316

479958LV00002B/404/P